Angel broke eye contact and fought the pain of an unreleased sigh.

She entered the yard, Brennan didn't follow. Her throat burned but there was nothing that could quench it, at least nothing Brennan was willing to offer. Well aware of his past, she shouldn't have allowed her hopes to rise.

Her fingers trailed the top of the gate. Brennan's hand caught hers and pulled the gate closed, drawing them together from either side.

He toyed with a wayward curl near the nape of her neck. "And don't trust your heart to Cecil."

Surprised, she inhaled sharply.

Brennan's eyes darkened as his hands wrapped around her arms and tilted her forward. Angel willingly followed his lead, her lips aching for the contact. Like a searing brand his mouth touched hers, igniting a flame deep inside her heart.

Books by Regina Tittel

Abandoned Hearts

Unexpected Kiss

Coveted Bride

Cherished Stranger

Devoted Mission

Love for Lenore

Rivalry & Romance

Fourth Time's the Charm

Regina Tittel

FOURTH TIME'S A CHARM

Published by Regina Tittel
Copyright © 2014 by Regina Tittel
Cover design by Regina Tittel

All Scripture quotations are taken from the King James Version.

ISBN-10: 0-9889002-7-0
ISBN-13: 978-0-9889002-7-1

Regina Tittel's books are written to uplift and encourage each individual while also entertaining them with a great story.

And it shall come to pass in the last days, saith God, I will pour out of my Spirit upon all flesh: and your sons and your daughters shall prophesy and your young men shall see visions, and your old men shall dream dreams. –Acts 2:17

Thank you to my wonderful friends and fellow authors in this series, Linda Cushman—One Rusty Spur, Mildred Colvin and Jonathan Colvin—Two Lonely Hearts, Jamie Adams—Three in a Quandary. You've all been a joy and a blessing in my life!

Thank you to my husband—you're still every hero I pen.

And thank you, God, for supplying me with a spiritual message for every book.

Chapter One

Warsaw, MO 1901

A shot rang out and echoed off the bluffs running along the river. Brennan Douglas reached for the loaded rifle encased beside him and listened for a recurring blast. Moments later another shot sounded, followed by the shrill scream of a horse. He kicked his heels into the sides of his mount and tore through the knee-high grass.

A thick forest of trees ran along the top of the hundred foot tall bluff. Brennan neared the shaded canopy before slowing his buckskin to a cautious gait. No movement. No sound. Animals had scurried to their dens. Birds sought safety in the treetops. He pressed though the eerie silence, unaffected by the thickened atmosphere.

Could it be the thieves from the recent bank heists? As sheriff of Warsaw, Brennan hoped so. The report from Lincoln said the men trailed his direction but disappeared around the river.

A blur of movement cut through the oak and sycamore stand across the river's bluff. Brennan reined his horse to a halt. He searched his saddlebag for the tortoise shell opera glasses he'd received in a trade. Though a bit fancy for his taste, they'd proven indispensable.

He focused the lenses, but with the distance, coupled with the approaching evening, nothing could be seen through the accumulating darkness but the outlines of trees and scrub.

Too bad this wasn't the inlet. He'd never make it around the river in time to apprehend the suspect. He clicked his tongue and Buck responded by nearing the edge.

Brennan scanned the area. No movement, no ripples in the water, no voices.

Another empty day.

***

After rounding a dozen cattle out of town and into a temporary hold, Brennan returned to the jail house with most of the morning spent. What was wrong with the farmers that they couldn't keep their animals corralled? He sketched a note of the brand and set it aside on his desk. Brennan stood and stretched his back then retrieved the paper again to make another note. *New fine to be administered for livestock not corralled.* He'd talk to the city council as soon as he found the time.

Brennan looked up as his deputy returned from scoping the river. "Find anything?"

"Nothing but the sun and, boy, is it hot." He swiped his brow with his forearm, tilting his hat further back on his head. The man's stomach growled loud enough to hear. His wide smile matched the friendly position of his Stetson. "Sis said they were serving fried rabbit today."

Brennan returned his smile easily. Only a couple years younger than the sheriff, twenty-five year old Colton Reese had two hollow legs. The man could eat a full steer and still be hungry—and lean. "This place isn't holding me back. Let's go."

They strolled through town to Meyer's Place, the best restaurant for miles. Both men took their usual table inside.

Colton's sister, Angela, weaved through tables and chairs in their direction. Blonde hair and fair skinned, most folks called her Angel. In her soft, soprano voice, she asked the usual, "What can I get you gentleman?"

"You already know what I want. Just what you told me this morning." Colton patted his stomach.

She frowned. "I'm sorry, Colton, I had my days mixed up. I told you tomorrow's special. Today it's ham and beans."

This suited Brennan fine. "Then bring us two plates, Angel." His nod at Colton said, like it or not, that's what's being served.

"I'm glad you're so easy to please, Sheriff. Wish my brother was half as much." As she turned to leave, the light caught the dimples in her cheeks revealing her teasing nature.

Colton leaned back with his arms crossed over his chest. "I suppose it's one of your favorite meals, growing up in a house full the way you did."

"We ate what our folks could afford and learned not to complain."

Colton stared toward the kitchen, his mouth pulled to the side, probably debating calling his sister back to change his order.

9

In the end, he must've chosen not to complain and changed the subject. "Hit me with the facts again, Brennan." Colton spoke quiet enough not to be overheard.

Brennan laid out the story he'd recapped in his own mind several times today. Three gunmen hit Edwards in bright daylight. Storming in through the front door with their heels on fire, they'd blasted off several shots into the ceiling and one above the tellers head, frightening every woman and child into a state of frenzy. Loud and brash, the tallest of the three demanded the money while the other two kept watch and generally harassed the bank's patrons.

"Why does Sheriff Douglas think they're the same gang?"

Although Brennan shared the same last name of Lincoln's sheriff they were of no immediate kin. And to lessen confusion, Brennan chose to go by his given name.

Colton continued, "The hold ups in Gravois Mills and Lincoln were completely different."

The fact seemed obvious to Brennan as well, almost too obvious. He leaned toward agreeing with Sheriff Douglas. The Gravois Mills bank was robbed in the early morning. The felon, of medium build, waited and watched for the banker to arrive then single handedly affronted him from the back of the building at gun point then helped himself to the safe. All in a gentlemanly manner, if that were possible.

The third robbery, just north in Lincoln, was the most extravagant. At the same time someone blew up the telegrapher's office, two men stormed the bank at closing and emptied the town's accounts.

Refined gentleman verses three obnoxious thugs. One man versus two. Too obvious and too close together. Someone was trying hard to confuse the surrounding lawmen. If it weren't for the sighting of the tall man in Lincoln the night before the heist, the three crimes may have never been connected. But at six foot six, the blond-haired stranger stood out like a streetlamp.

"You know the facts as well as I do. Think about it a while longer yet." Brennan didn't like to do Colton's thinking for him. If he was serious about a career in law, he'd profit from learning how to build a case on his own.

A scowl covered Colton's face as he tried to connect the robberies. At least he was trying.

Brennan considered the man who'd filled the role of deputy for the past two years. Colton's sense of responsibility to his sisters weighed heavily on him. Although grown, they still looked to their brother for guidance. The oldest had married after the first year of their parent's death. The youngest was now engaged which would leave only Angel at home. Once they all married, Colton would probably follow suit and settle down to farm. He was a good man, but his heart wasn't in law.

Brennan scanned the room, something he did incessantly. Years as a lawmen taught him to never trust his surroundings. Since they'd arrived after the lunch crowd most of the tables were empty save for those, like him and Colton, that'd worked through the heat.

11

A long-legged ranch hand strutted toward the cash register. "So what of it, Angel face? You gonna let me court ya or not?"

Although he'd never considered why, Brennan always tensed when witnessing a man flirt with the attractive waitress. He held his breath and listened for her response.

Colton emptied his water glass. "If the robberies are connected ..." His words died away as he followed Brennan's hardened stare to his sister and Dalton.

"Dalton, harassing me has never done you any good. Now get back to those calves. I can hear them bawling all the way in here."

Angel, good-natured to a fault, turned her back and slipped behind the door to the kitchen. The sour-faced cowpoke strode toward the street, his swagger less pronounced than before.

Brennan breathed easier. Good call, Angel. He didn't deserve you.

A tiny flame of jealousy warmed his blood. Still, she wasn't what he considered a good pick for a sheriff's wife. Trouble had a way of following Angela Reese and Brennan had enough of his own.

Colton stood, grabbed his hat and pulled the brim low over his eyes. Brennan didn't have to guess his actions. Their discussion of the robberies would continue later. Colton met the ranch hand by the front of the establishment and followed him out. He was as protective of his sisters as he was particular about who they spent time with. Not just anyone was allowed to court them, especially if they didn't have the good sense to go through him first.

Brennan scrutinized the room for any other would-be suitors. Angel's combined beauty and naive personality drew more than a normal amount of interest, and not all of them gentleman. For Colton's sake, he wished she'd find someone and settle down. Her brother would have a lot less worrying to do.

One of the ranchers left in the room met the sheriff's gaze with a challenge. Like the other man, Brennan recognized him from the Holt farm.

At ease with himself and his surroundings, the sheriff didn't flinch. If the man wanted trouble, he'd addressed the right person. "You got something to say?"

The man flexed his jaw before the brewing storm in his eyes simmered to a temporary calm. "Not today, Sheriff." His comment hinted of future conflict.

Angel, Angel. She attracted trouble like dust to cowboys.

***

Angel usually enjoyed her days off work, but the further she walked, the more she wished she was waiting tables instead. Door hinges squeaked as her older sister Clara entered the local mercantile. They'd already visited four other stores, and she could tell by her sister's mood she was tiring.

"Angela, at least give the poor guy a chance. Cecil would make a nice husband."

If she counted Dalton's sloppy attempt from yesterday, this made the fourth man to try to court her this week. Although not all of them had a serious relationship in mind, Angel knew Cecil as a gentleman. He wouldn't make an offer he didn't intend to stand behind. But his short, stocky frame didn't match the man from her dreams.

She answered Clara in the reflection of the mirror. "I already told you who I'm going to marry. I don't need to be wasting my time, or anybody's heart, on false pretenses."

"You mean you've seen his face?"

"What?"

"The man in your dream. You said you already told me who, but I don't recall, so that must mean you've seen his face." Clara dropped the gown she'd held against her and turned from the mirror with a hand on her amble hip. Pregnant and nearing her due date, her sister's patience was thinner than usual.

"No, I haven't, but God will reveal him in time." Angel covered her mouth with her hand and tried not to giggle. The gown hadn't fallen but rested across her sister's protruding stomach.

"Oh, dandelions and field mice have more sense than you! You can't base your whole future on a dream."

"Dreams," Angel corrected and replaced the garment on the rack. She understood how hard it was to believe. For over a year she'd dreamed of her future husband, yet never saw his face. "It takes faith to accept, Clara."

Clara turned her back and mumbled something about sensibilities, leaving the mercantile without a purchase. They had to decide on the perfect wedding present for Emma and soon. If too much time passed, Clara's condition would prevent her from shopping.

"Oh, look what Mia has in her window." Both girls crossed the street to the other shop. The mannequin sported a bold green suit jacket and skirt—the latest fashion with its full, low chest and curvy hips. Perched on her head sat a matching green velvet hat with a narrow brim. "Are you thinking what I'm thinking?"

Clara frowned. "I hope not. That would mean I base my future on dreams and not reality."

Angel swallowed and turned back to the window. God had spoken to Joseph in dreams, yet Clara didn't mock his story. And in the same method, God spoke to Gideon and Solomon and numerous others in the Bible. The book of Acts even prophesized that people would have visions and dreams.

She didn't expect Clara to support her, but her mule-like attitude wasn't pulling her any favors. Just because Cecil was Clara's brother-in-law didn't mean Angel had to marry him. "I meant that the hat would go well with the green assemble from Emma's wardrobe."

"If you want to buy our little sister a hat for a wedding present, do so, but don't expect me to pitch in." She waddled further along the boardwalk. "Imagine—a hat for a wedding present!"

Angel swallowed the building lump in her throat and followed several steps behind. She inhaled a deep breath. Life was too short to allow little nuisances to bother her. Whenever she did marry and have children, she hoped it didn't affect her personality the way it had Clara's.

"I have to stop." Clara eased onto a bench.

They'd walked toward the end of the boardwalk. The store wasn't Stinson and Freeman's department store, but there might be something worth regarding. "You rest and I'll look around in here." The sign read, The Right Place. Angel pushed as someone opened the door from inside. She stumbled forward … and into Sheriff Brennan.

Chapter Two

"Sheriff! Oh, excuse me." Angel righted herself from Brennan's arms as a flush climbed her neck to her face. She pressed a hand to her cheek. When did she ever blush?

His handsome face stretched into a smile as his deep voice invited her in. "Guess you weren't expecting door service." He moved to the side to allow her entrance. "Any trouble today?"

"No, today's my day off." Always watching out for others' safety, Brennan's protective nature made him popular with the whole town. "Clara and I are shopping for Emma's wedding present."

"Thinking about a rocking chair?"

Angel let her gaze follow the Sheriff's to the front window. She'd overlooked the display from outside. "Those are lovely."

"I have more upstairs if'n you'd like to take a look, Miss." Mr. Fremont, the owner, moved from behind the counter toward the back of the store.

Angel turned from him to Sheriff Brennan. "I think I'll see what he has in stock."

"I'll follow. Maybe a rocker on my front porch would attract a buyer. Something needs to help the house sell."

Angel climbed the stairs with the sheriff behind her. "I've always loved your home. Why I'd buy it myself if I could."

"Maybe you'll get to once you settle down. From the amount of interest it's stirred, it'll probably still be for sale."

She said nothing in response. Clara had spoken enough on the matter of marriage for one day.

Mr. Fremont was already seated when they reached the top. A little out of breath, he slapped the upholstered arm of his chair. "These just came in. If it's a wedding present you're after, this would be far finer than a plain wooden one."

Angel sat in the one next to the store owner. "Ahh." She relaxed against the soft back. "Even though I prefer the typical wooden rockers, this is nice."

She pushed off the floor with her toes and closed her eyes. When she opened them, Sheriff Brennan stood studying her.

"You look good resting in that chair. In fact, you might find settling down more pleasing than working at the restaurant."

A surge of annoyance had her feet planted on the floor, leaving the chair rocking heavily behind her. "What is it with everyone trying to marry me off? If I didn't know better I'd think the whole town was conspiring against me."

She turned to the surprised Mr. Fremont. "I'll talk to my sister and stop by later."

The sheriff's footsteps followed her down the stairs. "Angel, now don't get all riled up. I didn't mean to upset you."

Angel stopped by a displayed oak table as shame heated her face. Although she hadn't wanted to acknowledge the hurt, Clara's careless words had slid under her skin like a bothersome splinter. But that didn't excuse Angel's prickly attitude toward the sheriff.

She ran a hand over the smooth finish of the table top and said, "It's not just you. Clara hasn't been herself lately and that wears on me. I'm sorry for losing my temper."

"It's nice to know you can raise that little voice of yours." He motioned for her to go before him.

Angel swept past as he held the door open. "I will marry someday, Sheriff. Once I know who he is."

Sheriff Brennan raised an eyebrow before Clara lumbered to her feet. "We need to get going. Nice to see you, Sheriff." Clara's hand tightened around Angel's arm as they took off in a brisk walk.

"The rest must have really helped." Angel hurried alongside her sister. "This is practically running for you."

They slowed as they approached the buggy. Angel helped Clara climb up before taking the reins. Her sister's sudden silence surprised her. "Are you feeling well?"

"You were about to tell the sheriff your dreams, weren't you?"

Angel chanced a sideways glimpse. Based on the scowl Clara currently wore, it would've been a bad idea. "Why would that be wrong?" She braced herself for her disapproval.

"You don't want … everyone thinks … you need to keep a wise reputation about yourself." Clara sighed and gazed heavenward. "There are some things in life that are better kept private. Dreams are one of them."

Nothing else was said for the duration of the ride. After leaving Clara at her house, Angel directed the buggy toward home. Her mood waned. It was nice of Clara to try, but Angel knew what was left unsaid. People didn't see her as smart. Friendly, yes. Even fun to be around. But if her dream was made known they'd laugh her to scorn, which would bring embarrassment to Clara.

Okay, God. So I have to keep this one between us … and Emma. Oh, I've already told Colton, too. Wait, I did confide in Mrs. Meyer, the cook.

Angel unharnessed the horse from the wagon and sagged against the barn. She was hopeless.

She stepped through the back door of the house and into the comforting smell of freshly baked bread. "Oh, Emma, Todd is going to be one happy husband."

Emma spun around from the oven with a jubilant smile. "Only two more weeks and I'll be Mrs. Todd Davis!"

Angel laughed and joined her sister's enthusiastic mood.

"Did you and Clara pick out my wedding gift?"

Angel stilled. "You weren't supposed to know what we were up to."

"How could I not? When do the two of you go shopping together?"

"True. Well, we are closer to a decision than we were before we left." Although they still hadn't agreed on a purchase, the idea of a hat had definitely been eliminated.

A knock sounded from the front door. Angel took one look at her sister's dough covered hands and said, "I'll see to it." Through the window she saw her best friend, Juliann Hall.

"This is a nice surprise. Come on in."

Juliann entered with a gift beneath her arm. "I brought Emma's wedding present."

"Wedding present? Did I hear someone say they brought me a gift?" Emma wiped her hands on her apron, dropping a trail of dried bread dough.

Juliann laughed and shared a knowing look with Angel. Marriage would never change Emma. She'd always be the perfect representation of excitement and youth. Ever since they were children, Emma tagged along with them, keeping her presence known through acts of whimsy and imaginary adventures.

"Are you sure it's wise to leave it here? I don't think Emma can be trusted not to open the gift." Angel winked at her little sister.

"It's to open now." Juliann held out the tea cloth wrapped box. "She'll need it before her wedding."

Emma's excitement was contagious as Angel watched her fold back the towel. A gasp of air sucked through Emma's lips. "Your veil?"

Angel's eyes dampened as she admired the veil with its iridescent beads. Julie's kindness knew no end.

"You know the saying, something old, something new, something borrowed ..." She lifted the flimsy train. "This is a borrow. And soon, maybe Angel will be borrowing it, too."

Angel cringed. *Add another to the list, God.* She'd told Julie, too.

***

Brennan moved the wooden rocking chairs closer to the door and stood back to inspect the small change. He nodded his head in approval. The chairs added a friendly atmosphere. Surely that would speed up the sale of the over-sized house.

His decision made, why did he still feel restless and on edge? As if in answer, an image of Angel's pretty mouth tightened in a harsh line intruded on his thoughts. He should know better than to talk to women.

His thoughts trailed back through the last couple of years. His experience proved he didn't know what he was doing. What he thought was normal conversation was interpreted by them as bossy and arrogant.

Regret settled in his abdomen. He'd dealt with the rejection of Juliann and Sara, now cousins by marriage. But he didn't like to think of Angel feeling the same way. Brennan removed his hat and ran a hand through his hair. He'd make it up to her. Somehow.

With the jail locked for the evening and too restless to stay home, Brennan set off for the river. He still had three hours of daylight and although his deputy hadn't discovered any clues yesterday, Brennan found it paid to be overly precise.

He studied the ground, the branches, everything he could see as he rode. If the bandits hadn't come this far, where did they go? Up ahead, a rabbit hopped across the path and disappeared into a thicket. Similar to the furry rodent, the men might have chosen a concealed camp until enough time passed they could slip by. Surviving along the river didn't require a lot of skill.

The thought didn't bode well. They could be camped in any number of places

His horse cut a path through the knee-high grass. Despite the late hour in the day, the July sun sent sweat trickling past Brennan's temples as waves of heat swayed upward from the grain-filled tips. Not even the breeze made from their fast pace offered relief.

Buck, his reluctant ride, tired quickly. Brennan urged him to keep up a worthy pace. They'd soon come to the inlet where the horse could refresh himself.

The Osage River, filled with fish, waterfowl and barges, teamed with life. But also made for a crafty place to hide. With its many branches, it framed Warsaw on every side but the north. Buck snorted and slowed to a walk. Brennan would be grateful for a lead ... and a more dependable steed.

Determined horseflies swarmed the air along with their persistent cousins, the deerfly. Buck swung his tail and whipped Brennan's thigh. Tangled in the long horse hair, a piece of briar caught Brennan's hand and raked across his skin. He didn't flinch.

Raised on the outside of town with a half dozen siblings, Brennan had endured far worse than thorns. He'd been knocked around, shot, and drug behind a horse for half a mile all while still living at home as a rambunctious youth. Resisting the call of Christ, he left a wake of mischievous havoc wherever he went.

But after becoming a young man, he witnessed a devilish act against the Indians by a couple of reckless horsemen. Unable to stop them, yet haunted by the scene, Brennan changed. Accepting Christ had been the first step. Next, had been earning his badge.

A fly landed on his neck and bit hard. He shook off the pesky insect. They were thick as thieves. His horse tossed his mane. The flies were friendly with him, too. Buck quickened to a trot eager to return to the cool shade of the trees.

Nearing the inlet, Brennan allowed his stead to weave through the wooded patch at his own pace while he kept a sharp eye for signs of recent passage. With the exception of an occasional tuft of hair left by a deer, the forest withheld any clues.

Rocks lay scattered from the bluff to the edge of the water. Buck's hooves kicked up several as he lazily plodded along. If anyone hid nearby, they were now aware of his company.

While Buck took a nosily slurp of water, Brennan dismounted and wet his bandana then slapped it against the back of his neck. The small inlet wasn't wide enough for a river barge, but would certainly prove a worthy place to shove off with a smaller craft.

On the other side, tracks marred the smooth surface of the muddy bank. Brennan tensed, aware of the numerous places one could hide and watch. He scanned the perimeter. Nothing appeared sinister. A red-winged blackbird sang from his cattail perch as turtles sunned on a protruding log.

Based on Lincoln's report, Brennan half expected to discover tracks of a skiff that'd been hidden in the brush, but so far his only find was a load of beggar's lice. He'd pay the livery boy extra for combing them out.

Brennan wet his thirst with his canteen then rounded the inlet. The mud ran in two separate paths, disappearing at the water's edge. He removed his hat and ran his hand through sweat dampened hair. Thieves didn't leave webbed prints.

Maybe the men were further north. They'd worked their way from Edwards southeast of Warsaw, then to Gravois Mills to the east, before hitting Lincoln. The neighboring town's sheriff seemed convinced they'd complete their circle and drop south again to Warsaw. Brennan's jaw flexed. His town wasn't the wealthy trading post it used to be, but for the time it had been, it'd made a lot of men rich. Hitting the bank would be like striking gold. If the thieves pulled off a heist without getting caught, they'd disappear down the Osage River without a trace.

He rode through the trees climbing the bluff. Near the top, Buck shied and released a nervous whinny. Brennan's thighs tightened against his mount. He whipped his head around and slid his rifle from its pouch.

25

The excitement of the unknown increased his heart rate. Confident, and perhaps a little cocky, he braced himself for an attack.

Branches snapped. Leaves rustled. Something heavy moved their way. His rifle held ready to fire, Brennan kept a steady bead aimed forward.

A riderless horse limped into view.

Disappointment eased his taunt muscles. He'd expected a thief and a battle, not an injured animal. Cautious, Brennan slid to the ground and approached the helpless mare. A bullet had left a clean groove across the shoulder of her foreleg. Brennan grimaced at the swollen, tender muscle.

He checked the mare's other side then rubbed a hand down her spotted roan neck. Smooth and soft, her coat boasted of excellent care. Someone who spent this much time with their horse wouldn't leave it wounded in the woods. Either the mare had been stolen, or worse, her owner had also been shot.

The worn and outdated saddle lacked the typical embossed engravings. A poor man's horse? Without saddle bags there was no way to tell of the owner.

Brennan secured both horses to a tree and followed the mare's path. It didn't take long to find his second clue. Parallel to where he'd stood across the bluff the day before, hung a tangled mass of long hair. He frowned as he approached the tree. The injured mare's mane and tail were black. This hair was red.

As long as Buck's tail, Brennan assumed the hair belonged to a horse. He stretched a hand out. Soft … like a woman's.

Chapter Three

Angel stood on the back stoop outside the restaurant and inhaled the warm evening air. It wasn't often her shift ended early enough to enjoy what was left of the day. With only a few customers left, Mr. and Mrs. Meyer had decided to close early.

The only problem, Angel realized as she emerged from the alley to the boardwalk, was Emma didn't know to bring the buckboard into town early. Angel would have to walk home.

Her feet tapped against the boardwalk as the jingle of a wagon rolled by. Shops hummed with the voices of patrons. Angel enjoyed the comforts of town, much more than living on the farm.

In the window of Stinson and Freeman's, displayed on gingham covered stacked crates, sat the latest edition of cookery. Angel stopped and read the ad, "Agate nickel-steel ware." A chemist certificate was stamped to the side of the name stating the items to be free of arsenic, antimony, and lead. She admired the smooth surface of the porcelain pots and pans until she noticed the price. Clutching her reticule a bit tighter, she continued down the block. Thankfully she didn't need to consider the items as a gift. Emma's soon to be mother-in-law had already taken care of that.

On a whim, she chose not to cross the street, but covered a couple more blocks until she stood opposite of Sheriff Brennan's house. The white two-story home, surrounded by a picket fence, fueled her dreams. She leaned against a beam on the boardwalk and pretended to search through her reticule, while she put to memory each window, angle, and curve of the house, trying to imagine the home as hers.

In the front room, lace curtains would float across a floral chair as a breeze blew in from an open window. She imagined her bedroom off to the right. The cherry furniture would shine from the oil she'd rub on it each week. Her mother and father's log cabin quilt would blanket the bed and she'd crochet a fresh doily for the night stand.

Pale yellow would brighten the kitchen walls, welcoming the joy of sunshine. Sunflowers growing outside the window could decorate her table each week they were in bloom.

A laugh almost escaped her as her daydream escalated. But no one had to know. Unlike her dreams of her future husband, this one wasn't something she wanted to share.

Her fingers grazed the small roll of bills she'd earned this week. Little by little, her savings increased. Although it was highly unusual for a single woman, Angel hoped to buy the home herself. Waiting for God to reveal her husband was one thing, but that didn't mean she had to wait on her house.

***

Brennan arrived at his office the next morning with Colton minutes behind him. He took his turn at feeding the prisoners before joining his deputy in the office. After hanging his hat on the peg behind his desk, Brennan withdrew the wad of red hair from his pocket. "What do you make of this?"

Colton whistled as he unrolled the strands. "I'd say some poor woman's suffering a tender head." He left the hair on Brennan's desk and shot a quick glimpse at the sheriff then shuffled his feet.

Brennan grimaced. Something else was going on. "What is it? Do you know who this belongs to?"

"I wish that were all." Colton heaved a sigh and shook his head. "I'm afraid it's far worse than that. Read the letter on your desk."

Beside the red strands sat a white envelope, addressed from Lincoln. Brennan had overlooked it when he came in. He slid his knife beneath the sealed flap and slit the envelope open.

Robbery imminent. Sending Deputy Harris to increase man power. Still lack a stinking telegraph machine.

Sheriff Douglas

A half smile tugged on Brennan's mouth. He related easily to Sheriff Douglas and considered the experienced lawman an older, grumpier version of himself.

He tapped the letter on his desk as the message of the note sunk in with a heavy dread. The town was growing restless with the current state of affairs. Along with cattle running lose tearing up property, petty larceny was on the rise. Women and gentlemen alike worried over their general safety. Talk had already begun with fingers pointed at Brennan.

How quickly people forgot what he'd done for their town. He ground his teeth until they hurt. He'd spent years cleaning up, even going so far as to organize a posse between neighboring county sheriffs. Together they'd arrested several bands of thieves and a notorious murderer that'd preyed on the towns for years. But none of that would matter if the bank was hit. Brennan's respectability would be ruined along with the town's businesses.

He splayed his hands on his desk and stared at nothing. "Harris ..." Brennan growled out the name with disdain. The man had a way of making a person's skin crawl. "How you'd know?"

Colton adjusted his hat. "Saw him in town when Thad gave me the letter."

"Well, I'm not sitting around my desk all day waiting for him to show up for duty." Brennan stormed for the door. "I've been called out to the Stevens' farm. Seems some of the Holt workers are causing trouble again, stealing chickens this time. You watch the—"

Brennan stared out the open door. Colton joined him watching Lincoln's lawman stroll through town.

As if aware of his audience, Harris turned and smiled. His perfect set of teeth shone like polished ivory. "Morning, Sheriff Brennan. Deputy Reese." He crossed the street.

Colton slipped out the door. "I'll deal with the ranchers." Whether or not Colton had a heart for law, he possessed enough sense to know which job to take.

Brennan flexed his jaw as Harris drew closer. Whatever Lincoln's sheriff saw in the man, had yet to impress Brennan.

"I've got a hatful of responsibilities today, so make it quick." Brennan rested a foot on his desk chair while the catalog-model lawman took Colton's empty seat.

"All business and no play makes for a grouchy sheriff." Harris's smile reminded Brennan of a character sketch of the devil he'd once seen in the newspaper.

"You didn't come all the way from Lincoln to waste my time. Now why does Sheriff Douglas think we'll be hit?"

Harris leaned forward as if in conspiracy with Brennan. "The tall one was overheard the night before the hit in Gravois Mills. He mentioned an interest in this forgotten town. Why?—I haven't the foggiest. I realize Warsaw used to be a hotbed of excitement, but since the riverboats gave way to the train … well, what more do I need to say?"

Sheriff Douglas could have easily mentioned the little bit of news in the letter. Why did he send his deputy? Brennan left his desk and stood with his feet apart in front of Harris. "And your business here is?" Brennan wasn't known as a patient man.

Harris leaned back with his hands behind his head. "The sheriff seems to hold a lot of respect for you and since you're understaffed, he took it upon himself to send me to help."

Brennan flipped the leg of the man's chair, sending him sprawling to the floor. "Then you can start anytime." He didn't bother to hide his smirk. In Brennan's opinion, Deputy Harris could use a few scuffs in his city-suited armor. The Kansas native dressed like a Bostonian. His confusion over his identity was enough to build distrust, but his cocky attitude was the real thorn. The man's constant barbs, both from today and their meetings in the past, seemed to hint of a personal vendetta against Brennan.

If that was the case, he could add chair tossing to the list.

***

"This here's T. J. Sanders." Brennan introduced Harris to the town's small-framed banker.

The banker finished tightening a stack of bills with repeated glances toward the newcomer.

"Sanders, this is Deputy Harris from Lincoln. He'll be helping us out for a *short* while. Says there's a probable hit planned for our bank."

Mr. Sanders pulled his reading spectacles further down his nose and glanced over the wire rims. "I've heard about the recent robberies in surrounding counties." His voice, though usually nasal and weak, came across sharp.

The man appeared worked up over something. Could it be Harris? Or more disgruntled talk about Warsaw's sheriff?

"Harris will give you a description of the men."

"What about the vault?" Harris peered around the barred window separating the cashier from the public.

Brennan resisted the urge to rub his palm across the handle of his sidearm. Something about Lincoln's deputy didn't add up. He chucked the thought away for now, but would definitely give it consideration once he had a moment alone.

"One thing at a time, Harris. Give the descriptions." Although the small task could've been carried out by either man, Harris had to feel he carried some importance. Otherwise, the debutant deputy might catch on Brennan didn't plan on sharing anything. Not with a man he couldn't trust.

The front door opened and in walked Mrs. Adams and her six children. Despite the obvious fact she was married, her raven black hair and soft features often drew the attention of strangers.

The description Harris had begun faded on his tongue as he smiled and stared at the new customer. He slid over to allow her use of the window, yet remained close enough to rob her of privacy.

Brennan yanked him back by the arm. "Allow the lady some room."

A nervous glance from Mrs. Adams confirmed he did the right thing. She drew her children closer. "Are we interrupting you, Sheriff?"

"Nothing that can't wait. We'll finish up after you."

Mr. Sanders worked quickly to fill her request. "Have a good day, Mrs. Adams. See you and the family in church Sunday."

And that's how it worked in Warsaw. Everyone knew their neighbor.

Brennan rubbed his chin and studied Harris. He seemed to leave a nervous wake with folks he met. If he'd try to be likable and earn their trust it would benefit the case. But ... perhaps he and Brennan were working the case from two different angles.

The door closed behind Mrs. Adams, once more, leaving the men alone.

Brennan glowered at Harris. "Wasn't there something else about the men? A distinguishing feature, or something about height?"

"Oh, yeah." Like a sly fox, even Harris' smirk couldn't hide his overabundance of teeth. At least with a fox, you knew to lock up your chickens. But what was this man hunting?

Harris leaned an elbow on the counter. "Yeah, there was a tall guy in one of the robberies. Oh, I'd say he wasn't much taller than you, Brennan."

"*Sheriff* Brennan." Brennan corrected. Only those close to him ever dropped the title.

***

The afternoon couldn't come quickly enough. Tired of his new side-kick, Brennan anticipated Colton's return more with each passing minute. He led Deputy Harris to the table Angel kept reserved for him and Colton.

Harris straightened his vest. The man had finally given up on his matching jacket. The heat was too high to be concerned with style. Brennan almost laughed before another thought doused his sense of humor. Harris' concern for his outward appearance could be for show. How much did Sheriff Douglas truly know about his deputy?

He'd worked for the town of Lincoln little more than a year. Aside from that, Brennan knew very little about the man. "You have family left in Kansas?"

Harris's eyes darted toward the sheriff before a muscle twitched in his jaw. "None."

Although he'd tried to cover his instant reaction, Brennan caught the small nuance. He probed further to make Harris think he hadn't noticed. "You have a family of your own in Lincoln?"

His gaze narrowed before his unnerving smile returned. He stared at Angel approaching their table. "Nah. No need."

Brennan tensed. To Harris, Angel was off-limits. Brennan would see to it, even if he had to toss him out on the street.

Angel stopped at their table with a pitcher of cold water. "Have you men decided on what you'll have?" She leaned forward to fill both glasses. Brennan didn't miss the deputy's interest. His hungry eyes took in more than his share.

Brennan stretched his legs beneath the table giving Harris a swift kick in the knee. He replied to his grunt, "Sorry about that. These short tables weren't made for a man of my length."

Angel took their order and moved to the next group of customers. Her too-trusting nature could land her in trouble one day. He rubbed his fingers against his palm, agitated by the thought. Brennan hoped he was there if it happened.

He turned his attention to Harris. "Now that you've seen the bank, based on the other robberies, how do you think they'll take this one?"

Before Harris could reply, the door swung open. Colton limped toward the table. As he neared, the lighting revealed a swollen lip and a cut beneath his eye.

Chapter Four

Brennan's fists curled on top of the table. "Looks like I'll be paying the Holts' a visit myself."

Colton straddled an empty chair and smiled around his swollen lip. "No need. Doc Haynes is on his way out there now."

"Haynes? Why—" Suddenly Brennan knew. Colton, out-numbered, had left the ranch hands in worse shape than himself. Pride for his deputy swelled his chest. "Well done. What caused the ruckus?"

"Dalton's sensitive nature. He didn't appreciate my disapproval of him. Add the chicken fiasco to the mix and it was more than he could take." He smiled and rubbed his jaw. "It was sorta fun. I'd do it again."

Angel's gasp interrupted Brennan's chuckle. "Colton!"

Colton rose from the table and ushered his sister toward the kitchen. His explanation could be heard as she fussed over his face.

Brennan's attention settled back on Harris. The smug expression he'd worn as Colton described his encounter with Dalton raised concern. What was it about the man? Even now, the way his lecherous eyes followed after Angel made the sheriff's neck bristle. Harris reminded him of a sleazy coyote on the prowl.

Hadn't he compared him to a fox earlier in the day? Was Brennan's opinion biased or did others see a similar reproach? He considered Angel, sweet and innocent. Suddenly irritated, he wanted to see the man back in Lincoln. "When you heading back?"

"I don't have immediate plans. The bank in Lincoln's already been emptied." Harris seemed too pleased with the situation.

Colton rejoined them at the table. "I told Sis to bring us each the special." He glanced between the Sheriff and Deputy Harris. "What plan did you come up with?"

"Nothing." Brennan hoped his tight-lipped response sent Colton the message not to share more than needed. A visit with Sheriff Douglas was in order. Brennan needed to learn all he could about the robberies and how long Warsaw was expected to tolerate Lincoln's deputy.

The diner filled up quickly as more patrons stopped in to enjoy Mrs. Meyer's skills. She possessed an equal talent in both desserts and dinner, assuring her savory creations always brought a constant crowd.

They finished their meal and Angel came back to address dessert. Harris smiled. His hungry expression looked like he hadn't seen a woman in weeks. "I'd like an angel on a cloud."

Angel's dimples appeared with her smile as she wagged a finger. "What would you men do without my name to tease me with?"

"I suppose they'd have to think." Brennan's retort came across short and gruff.

Like tiny bells the church used at Christmas time, Angel's laughter rippled sweetly across the table. "Thank you, Sheriff. Now if you're serious about that order, Deputy, I'll bring you a dish of Berries on a Cloud."

"Anything to keep you in my sights."

Angel shook her head as she turned back to the kitchen. Colton's eyes narrowed. "That's my sister you're admiring."

Harris simply shrugged.

"You should also know she's spoken for." Colton's chair scraped against the floor as he rose and spoke loud enough for Angel to hear from the back of the restaurant. "Cancel that order, Sis. We've got work to do."

Brennan's mouth pulled in a smirk as they rose to leave. When Colton took charge, he did so efficiently. Although Angel wasn't spoken for, Colton's idea had merit so long as Harris didn't demand to know the name of her supposed beau. Or worse, ask Angel before Colton had time to explain her recently changed social status.

Harris removed a rolled cigarette from a brass case inside his jacket pocket. "I hope I lost my dessert for a reason." He struck a match against the outside of the building and took several puffs on the end of the tobacco.

Brennan took the imperceptible nod from Colton to take over. The young deputy's plan had run its length. "We need to scout the surrounding countryside for a possible escape route should Warsaw be hit."

He still needed to connect with Sheriff Douglas. "I've got things to take care of. You two head west and since it'll be late by the time you return, report back to me in the morning."

"Why west?" Harris' question seemed innocent enough. Why then did Brennan think there was more behind it?

"If you were to rob the bank, what direction would afford you the quickest route out of here?"

"Me?" A trail of smoke streamed through wide nostrils. "Well, since we're playing pretend … I reckon I'd head south. It doesn't take a lot of wit to know most lawmen would head for the river. One could hop a train and be gone before you knew to change your course."

A distrustful aura lingered in the air. Though it might take a bit longer, the river also looped around the south end of Warsaw, and Brennan was certain Harris was aware of this. If he wanted to direct them a different direction then Brennan would take the bait, but only for the benefit of buying himself more time.

"Colton, I reckon he's right." He ignored Colton's raised brows. "Shoot south and search for any obvious trails and the best place to head off a party on the run."

***

Angel cleared another table before wiping a clean cloth across the top. Since the Meyers purchased the restaurant, business had steadily increased. Despite that fact, between lunch orders and friendly talk, Angel continued to see images of last night's dream. The vision always started with a stampede of cattle large enough to fill the town. The brays and snorts still sent a shudder down her arms. Dust circled the air, blinding her vision. Her feet felt leaden, her voice hoarse. And just when death's door seemed her last reprieve, strong arms would lock around her and pull her to safety.

What did it mean?

"Hi, sis."

"Hi, Emma. Todd. This is a nice surprise." Angel greeted her sister and soon-to-be brother-in-law as they entered, glad for their presence.

Todd returned her greeting with a smile then peered over the room. "You're quite busy today."

"Yes, we are. I hope Mr. Meyer finds extra help soon."

"If there's not an empty table we could eat at the boarding house."

"Take Colton and Sheriff Brennan's. They've already been in." Angel swiveled to serve another table of patrons and spoke over her shoulder. "I'll be with you in a moment."

Emma smiled jubilantly as she passed. She and Todd hadn't even wed and she already glowed. Angel's kid sister would make a lovely bride.

"I had the steak." The man's deep voice startled Angel from her musings. The plate teetered in her hand before the gentleman reached out. The dinnerware became engulfed in his large hand.

"Sorry about that. I got lost in thought." Suddenly nervous, Angel couldn't wait to get to her sister's table.

"Anyone could forgive a girl as pretty as you," spouted the tall man's companion.

"Um, thank you." She stole another quick glance at the man whose voice resembled a tuba from the town's marching band. Never had she seen someone's height while seated, nearly equal hers while standing.

"Sis," Emma met her at the counter and filled two glasses with water. Familiar with her sister's job, Emma often made herself comfortable, leaving very little for Angel to do for her. "We know what we want so I can tell you now." Her voice lowered to a whisper. "By the way, who's that gentleman you served?"

Angel couldn't resist a glance over her shoulder and wished Colton and Sheriff Brennan were still here, but they'd left before the strangers arrived. "He might be Goliath."

Emma stifled a giggle. "I always pictured Goliath with dark hair not blonde."

"Me, too." Angel cocked her head to the side and tapped her cheek, now calmer beside Emma. "But I bet he sounded like this man. His voice is so deep it's thick."

"I agree. I couldn't help overhear him." She lifted the filled glasses. "And I always thought Sheriff Brennan had a deep voice."

"Mm ... I know." His image came to mind, seated at the table by the wall, the dimples in his cheeks deepening as he shared something humorous with Colton.

"Angel?"

"Huh?" Angel refocused on her sister

A knowing smile formed across Emma's lips. "There's a bit of honey-glow on your cheeks. That wouldn't have anything to do with our sheriff, would it?"

Angel's breath stalled as her heartbeat quickened. She threw a hand to her face and spun around with her back to the room. "Oh, this can't happen?"

"What can't happen?"

"I can't develop feelings for the *sheriff*."

"Why not?" Emma demanded.

"I'm supposed to marry the man from my dreams. And that can't be Sheriff Brennan." She turned back and stared at the light streaming in from the door. "Why everyone knows what losing Juliann did to his heart. Not to mention the trouble he had when Sara came to town. I'm sure he's sworn off ever marrying."

***

Once the men were gone from sight, Brennan headed for the telegraph office. "How's it going, Robert?"

"Not bad if you can stand the heat." Robert Hall swiped the visor off his head, revealing a band of sweat dampened hair. Despite the open windows, there was no escape from the hot, humid air.

Robert had come to town two years prior searching for the woman who'd supposedly given him up for adoption and found not only had he been stolen instead of abandoned, but that he had a family larger than he'd ever imagined. A family that included Brennan's aunt as his mother.

Brennan hadn't taken to the man right off. Skeptical of his story and resenting Robert's attraction to Juliann, the woman Brennan thought he'd been courting, he hadn't been able to see past his own feelings to the hurt-filled man. It wasn't a time in his career he was proud of.

"Can I do something for you?"

Robert's voice pulled him back to the present. He focused on the efficient telegrapher, now proud to have him in the family. "Have you seen any new faces in town?" Brennan gave a short description of the wanted man.

"Can't say that I have. Nothing unusual has come through either." He patted the stack of wired messages.

Brennan wasn't surprised. Good leads took time and he'd just begun to work the case. "How long do you suppose it'll take for Lincoln to set up another telegraph office?"

"Depends when they can get another machine. I have an extra stored around here somewhere." Robert knelt to rummage under the counter. "Here it is. We could lend them this one."

"Perfect. Send your message boy to Thad. Tell him I said to stop by and pick it up." Brennan rubbed a hand across his stubbled jaw. "I need a way to communicate with Sheriff Douglas. And soon."

He'd prefer riding out to Lincoln and talking to the sheriff face to face, but something warned him not to turn his back on Warsaw. He slapped the required coins, plus a tip for the message boy, onto the counter. "Keep this between you and me."

"You betcha, Sheriff."

Brennan chuckled as he left and mounted his ride. Despite the growth of their friendship, their initial meeting had made a lasting impression on Robert. To this day, though mostly in humor, he still referred to Brennan as Sheriff.

Back in town Brennan pulled alongside another cousin, Daniel Douglas.

Daniel inquired, "Haven't seen you lately. Been busy?"

"Up to my neck."

"I know the feeling." Daniel glanced toward his office. "I'm trying to slow down. Sara wants me to shorten my hours. Speaking of which, we'd like to have you over. Maybe some time next week."

"Sounds good. Let me know."

They said goodbye and parted ways. Daniel had married Sara Jordan, Brennan's mail-order bride. Only Brennan had never made the order. Instead, two men determined to get even with the sheriff had played with the innocent woman's heart and future. Brennan was happy for Sara and Daniel. If not for her, Daniel's mother would have insisted he marry for pedigree over love, making a miserable man out of him.

Brennan nudged his buckskin into motion. Buck snorted and chewed the bit, but finally gave in to his master. Like every other horse Brennan owned since becoming sheriff, this one had his flaws. Stubborn and lazy, the buckskin would rather graze and grow fat than be of service.

A scattering of children played in a stretch of cleared land behind the businesses on Main Street.

Brennan nodded as he rode by. Childish pranks from his boyhood kept him aware of their mischievous tendencies. But today their game of tag appeared harmless.

A couple boys whispered to one another before pulling finger-guns from imaginative gun-belts. In unison, they yelled, "Bang! Bang!"

Brennan grabbed his chest and sunk forward in the saddle. The dramatics brought a cheer from the young group. "You kids be good. Don't want to lock any of you up."

"Aw, Sheriff, I'd brake otta yo'r jail in two seconds." A boy about the age of ten set his foot on a tree stump and chewed on a blade of grass.

"Yeah, me too," echoed one of his cohorts.

Brennan could remember feeling much the same way at that age—invincible. If weightier matters weren't at stake, he'd corral them to the jailhouse and let them test their skills. As it was, he'd already let enough time slip by.

He rode on toward the bank. The back of the brick and mortar building posed one additional weakness that the front lacked. Trees. A thin scattering of hardwoods started no more than ten yards away. Granted the forest wasn't thick, but it did provide concealment for someone intent on discretion.

But discretion could be played by both sides. He'd talk to a few members from church, men he trusted, and set up a round of watchmen. Situated in the trees, they would see or hear anyone approaching the back side of the bank. And from his porch, Brennan could keep an eye on the front.

He weaved through the woods and fought the reins as his horse tore at every mulberry branch within reach. "We'll never get to the river at this rate."

What seemed like hours later, Brennan slipped out of the saddle to stretch his legs and study the ground. His gelding stayed back, more intent on filling his stomach than his head.

Not far ahead wore a narrow path. The packed soil stretched from the same direction he'd trekked then continued toward the river. The tracks showed three horses had arrived from the river and then returned by the same route. Brennan traced his finger along the horseshoe shaped dirt. One of the horses carried a heavy load.

He remounted and weaved further away from the path to hide his tracks. Up ahead, the trees gave way to field and river bank. Clumps of cattails and river cane littered the water's edge. Something splashed and a horse nickered. "Don't answer that, Buck." Brennan kept his voice low.

He retrieved his binoculars from the saddle bag and focused across the river. The reeds shook before three men climbed onto the other side of the bank. Shirtless backs shined with droplets of water while their pants clung to their legs. What type of men had enough time to cool off in the middle of the day?

They left the water and stood on level ground. Then Brennan understood. Standing at least a foot taller than his cohorts, the blonde fit the description from Sheriff Douglas. Only he appeared several inches taller than Brennan had anticipated.

Buck pawed the ground, restless to reach another limb. Brennan couldn't risk exposure. The men undoubtedly stood near their gun-belts leaving the sheriff outnumbered three to one. If it hadn't been for Harris, Colton wouldn't be wasting his time in the wrong direction and they could've easily made the arrests. As it was, Brennan could do nothing but return to town.

Chapter Five

Angel extinguished the last light in the restaurant and followed the cook outside. Mr. Meyer had gone home earlier complaining of his back, leaving the women to close up alone. While Mrs. Meyer secured the building Angel glanced over her shoulder but saw nothing. The dusky light hid everything but the deepening shadows of late evening. A shiver raced up her spine despite the warmth of summer. Ever since she'd waited on the table of the tall stranger and his friend, a sense of dread hung over her like a ruined umbrella. Somewhere a storm was brewing. And something told her she was about to get wet.

An owl hooted from a nearby tree. Angel jumped and grabbed the cook's shoulder.

"Ah-h!" Mrs. Meyer startled beneath her sudden touch. "Angela Reese, what's gotten into you? Now I've dropped the key."

Angel felt along the steps where the key had plunked against the wood. Nerve endings tingled beneath her hair and a slight sweat broke along her brow. She already had to deal with her elder sister's disappointment. Angel didn't want her employer to find reason to feel the same.

"Found it." Relief coursed through her as she handed the key back to Mrs. Meyer.

"Good. I'm surprised my holler didn't rouse the Mister, but considering his pain level, he might be well-off to sleep."

"How long does a muscle strain take to heal?" The welcome conversation broke the quiet evening.

"Not long. He'll be back to 'imself in a couple days."

A stray cat meowed from beneath the steps and tentatively slipped out into the open. Angel bent down and stroked the soft furry head.

The lock turned with the jingle of the key. Mrs. Meyer shook her head and clicked her tongue. "You're just encouraging him to stay, you know?"

"If he's a good mouser, he might be what we need." A small moan escaped Angel as she straightened. She had nothing to complain about. Her muscles weren't pulled, just tired.

"I imagine your bones are aching by now. Poor girl, we'll find extra help soon."

"I don't mind. I'm glad business is doing well." Angel spoke the truth, though by tomorrow morning's early shift, she might be tempted to interview customers as she poured their coffee.

"Good night, child. You be careful now and hold your reticule with both hands. With all the thieving going on, you don't want anyone snatching it." Mrs. Meyer climbed the stairs behind the building next-door.

Angel's jaw stretched wide in an unladylike yawn. Too tired to bring her hand to cover her mouth, she was at once thankful for the late hour.

She'd spent a long day waiting tables and would only repeat the process again at sunrise. She shuffled her aching feet forward. Hopefully Colton waited on the street with the buck wagon.

"Good evening, Miss *Angelic* Reese."

Angel teetered to a stop at the end of the alley before stumbling into Deputy Harris. "Deputy, I didn't see you standing there ... in the middle of the walk." Had he positioned himself in her path on purpose?

"A nice girl like you should be escorted, not left alone."

His smile appeared bright even at dusk. How did he keep his teeth so white? Angel smiled at her silly thought and focused past him for Colton. Her brother was late.

Harris drew her arm through his and proceeded to turn the opposite direction of home.

"Forgive me, Deputy, if my smile misled you. I'm not in need of your services. My brother will be here for me."

A quiet moment passed as he studied her. He slid her hand into his and smiled again. The man sure had a lot to be happy about.

"You've worked hard all day. Wouldn't you like an evening of company?"

Angel frowned. It A lady wouldn't agree to spend unescorted time with a man at this hour. Perhaps he hadn't thought through his request, and if he had, he was in need of a church service not her company. She pulled her hand back and clutched her reticule in front of her. "Deputy Harris, I'm flattered by your attention, but if you mean to court me I'm not available."

Harris' chin dropped a fraction. "Yes, that's what your brother told me. But what kind of intended leaves you in the dark?"

She'd misread him, he was a gentleman after all. A flutter of relief lightened her thoughts. "If you're talking about my future husband, that's hard to answer."

"Why is that?"

"Because I only meet him in my dreams."

"What?" His ever-present grin dropped on one side.

"I know it sounds … unusual. But God will reveal him in His time."

Harris tipped his hat further back on his head and chuckled. "Now if that don't beat all."

"Angel." Colton's voice drew Angel's attention and an immediate guilt hardened her stomach.

She glanced back at Harris. She shouldn't have told him.

***

Brennan grabbed the boiling pot of coffee with a wadded cloth and filled his cup for the third time. Having spent half the night on the porch watching the bank left him moving slower than usual. But thanks to the cane-backed rocking chairs he'd purchased, the night hadn't been as uncomfortable as it might have otherwise.

He returned to the porch and stared at the two rockers, side by side. A picture of Angel filled the second chair. The sudden image both startled him and piqued his curiosity. Brennan had never considered keeping company with her before now. A lightness lifted his chest. There sure wasn't anyone sweeter. But before the thought had a chance to swell, bitter memories stole his musing. He'd been played the fool twice before. Which was exactly why the house was for sale. He'd be smart to leave it that way.

Brennan straightened from the porch railing. The sun began to rise, bathing the town in a light orange glow. He guided his thoughts toward work, a safer subject. Colton would be interested in the discovery he'd made at the river, but first Brennan had to distract Harris with another errand. His gut instinct still soured at the thought of trusting the Lincoln man.

Brennan tipped the last swallow of coffee. Time to start the day. His footsteps echoed through the sparse living room to the kitchen before he placed the cup upside down in the dry sink. A flicker of disappointment raced across his heart.

He'd built the home with hopes of sharing it with Juliann Hall and a bundle of future children. But somehow he'd lost her to his cousin. He still didn't understand what Robert had that he didn't.

Brennan returned outside. Situated near the far end of town, his house was two blocks from the jail house. Eager to start work and escape his dreary thoughts, he for once wished it was closer.

The bank sat across the street at the end of the block. Brennan watched it closely until turning the corner. Quiet and serene, the town had yet to wake from its slumber. Mornings like this were to be treasured. He glimpsed at the brightening sky.

"Guide my decisions today, Lord. I feel like this business with the bank robberies has me stumbling around in the dark. Reveal what I'm missing. Protect this town and the good people who call it home. They depend on me. And I sure don't want to let them down."

He passed the town's main restaurant as he neared the jail and thought of Angel.

As if she stepped from his thoughts, Angel emerged from the corner and lighted across the road. A thundering of hooves and the rattling of a wagon erupted through the empty streets. Brennan yanked his head around and watched in horror as a coach barreled toward her.

"Angel!" Her name tumbled past his lips as he hurled himself forward. Blue eyes riveted his direction before widening at the speeding horses. She froze in place. Her high pitched scream pierced the air.

Brennan reached Angel and swept her against his chest before stumbling to the side. His heart pounded with the deafening sound of the horses' hooves as they sped past in a cloud of dust. No doubt late for the train, the driver drove the neck-breaking speed to make up for lost time, but Brennan would insure the mistake wasn't made twice.

Angel could've been lost.

"Um … Sheriff Brennan."

"Oh, er …" Brennan loosened his hold that kept Angel pinned against him, though not willing to fully release her until his heart calmed. His concern grew at the sight of her colorless face. "Isn't it a mite early for you to be out? I thought you worked 'til closing last night?"

She brushed a wisp of hair from her face with a shaky hand and said, "I did, but we're short on help."

His mouth tilted at the sound of her airy voice. If he'd been a moment too late, he might have never heard the musical notes again.

He blinked to redirect his thoughts and turned to where the wagon disappeared around the next corner. Torn between finding the driver of the coach and seeing Angel safely to work, the dark circles beneath her eyes made his decision. Judging by her fatigue it was no wonder she hadn't noticed the horses.

Angel moved back as he dropped his hands and her shawl slipped from her shoulder. Brennan tried to right it, his large hands feeling clumsy against the dainty material.

Angel's hand brushed against his as she took the lacey film and repositioned it. Brennan's breath stalled for a brief moment before he brushed it off as a reaction to her near trampling.

"Come on, I'll see you across the street." He wanted to say more. Not to keep her company ... but to lecture her about overworking.

Despite his accusing conscience, that was the excuse he was willing to accept.

"Sheriff Brennan," Angel climbed onto the boardwalk, allowing them to stand eye to eye. A twinkle flashed in her light green gaze. "Did you just save my life?"

Brennan's collar grew warm under her scrutiny. He glanced to the street and back. "I guess so."

A peculiar expression claimed her pretty face. Her eyes no longer appeared as shadowed. Her mouth pulled in an appealing grin. "Hmm … that's what I thought."

***

Once Angel disappeared inside the diner, Brennan hurried to the stall behind the jailhouse. Without taking time for a saddle, he threw a leg over Buck and tore off in the direction of the coach.

Fresh from the barn, Buck easily caught up with the exhausted horses. Brennan pulled alongside the driver and Thad Hackings drew the horses to a quick halt. The overworked animals tossed their heads, flinging foam from their thirsty mouths across Buck's head and neck. "What's your hurry, Thad?"

"Miz Louis can't miss this here train," Thad continued, seemingly unaware of his near rundown of Angela Reese, "and we got off on a late start with the hold up and all—"

"Hold up?" Brennan pulled on his reins and urged Buck to back up. Inside the coach sat a woman in her early twenties at best, dressed in plain clothing with her hair slung over one shoulder. Long, red hair.

"Were you hurt, Ma'am?"

"No, sir." The woman's eyes settled on anything but his.

"What was stolen?"

She bit her lip and refused to answer.

"They's just interested in her small satchel. They rummaged through ever'thing, and when they found the satchel, that's all they took, Sher'ff." Thad heaved a shoulder and chucked his chin toward the coach. "Seems to me they knew what they's a look'n fir."

"That's peculiar."

Thad motioned with his hand for Brennan to come closer. The sheriff nudged Buck forward. "I heard one of 'em say some'in 'bout teaching her a lesson. But the one in charge said they couldn't get messy, not when they're so close. Whada'ya think they meant?"

Brennan didn't know, but he was certain the woman in the coach did.

"What's your name, ma'am?"

A voice barely choked out an answer, "Sa— Cynthia Louis."

"Did you know these men?"

The train whistled around the corner before the chugging of wheels signaled its departure. The woman's demeanor crumpled as she lost herself in a fit of tears. Brennan circled the air with his finger, "Bring it around, Thad. No one's leaving anywhere just yet."

***

Choosing the comforts of Meyer's Restaurant over the jail house office, Brennan settled the young lady at his usual table then spoke with Angel near the kitchen. "Fix her a plate of eggs and bacon. I figure she could use a good meal."

Angel's eyes filled with concern as they centered on her first customer of the day. "Would she like a glass of fresh orange juice?"

"Cynthia," Brennan called her by her given name for a reason. Just as he suspected, she didn't flinch. "Miss Louis."

The woman jumped in her seat as if hearing him for the first time. Large, round eyes met his.

"Angel wondered if you'd like a glass of juice with your breakfast?" Brennan left Angel's side and moved toward the table.

Miss Louis fidgeted with the hem of the table cloth and nodded. "Yes, sir ... and ma'am."

Though not quite southern, the newcomer spoke with a twang not common to Warsaw. Questions swarmed Brennan's mind faster than cowpokes to Mrs. Meyer's pies. He cleared his throat as he took a seat and leaned his arms on the table. "If you're name's not Cynthia, what is it?"

"Huh? How—how'd ya know?" Her eyes darted toward the door. "I didn't do nothin' wrong. And I ain't goin' to no jail."

"If I wanted you behind bars, you'd already be there."

Her slack jaw meant his authoritative voice had proven his point. She ran a nervous tongue over her lips. "I am Miss Louis. My first name is Savannah."

"Save me the trouble of fishing for answers and tell me your story."

"My story?"

"Everyone has a story." Brennan rested an elbow across the back of the chair and relaxed. "Where did you come from? Why are you running?" He withheld the question forefront on his mind. What about the satchel?

"I'm not running ... at least I wasn't." Her shoulders heaved with a sigh. "My aunt took a fall, and I was sent to help with the kids 'til she healed up."

"Where was this?"

"North of Lincoln. A mean-spirited yearling broke her leg and with so many youngun's, you understand, she couldn't manage with Uncle Bill workin'. And it's not that he didn't try. He's a real good man ..."

Despite his impatience, Brennan forced himself not to rush the woman. Answers came easiest when folks were relaxed. He'd allow a few minutes more before redirecting her to the subject at hand.

"... and that's how come I was at the river ..."

Brennan blinked and refocused.

"With Aunt Ellie healed up there was no sense in my staying, but that didn't mean I had to hurry home. So like I said, at the river while Whinny was resting herself, I stretched my legs and ventured around. And that's when I found the little cave." Her voice dropped in volume. "And an old satchel."

"What was in it?"

She shrugged as if it was of little interest. "Just some money and some papers."

"*Some* money?"

"It wasn't that big of a bag."

"What kind of papers?"

"I dunno." Savannah scrunched up her face in thought. "There was lists with some of the lines marked through. But even though I can read a little, I didn't take the time. I started gettin' nervous."

She leaned forward. "When I opened it and saw the cash, I knew I'd probably stumbled onto some of that stolen money I heard about. So I carried the satchel back to Whinny, hefted it onto the saddle with me and figured I could return it and earn a reward."

Skepticism narrowed Brennan's eyes.

Savannah clamped her mouth together so tight her lips lost their color.

"What? Go on."

"Nope." She crossed her arms in front of her and whipped her head to the side. "There's no need if you think I'm a liar."

Brennan tongued his cheek. She had a point. "Then make me a believer. Where did you hop aboard Thad's coach?"

She swallowed and a look of sadness washed over her. Unlike most people, she didn't shake it off or try to hide it. "To tell that, I have to tell about Whinny."

"Whinny's your horse?"

"Yeah. We started off through the woods and someone hollered real angry. I didn't know who it was, but I wasn't going to stick around and find out. I kicked my heels in Whinny and urged her up the side of the bluff. But … he shot …" she sniffled. "Anyway, I grabbed the bag and my pack and ran 'til I got tired. In the morning I continued back toward Lincoln and that's when I caught the coach heading south.

"I really did figure I'd turn the satchel in here at Warsaw. Only … now I don't have it."

Dishes rattled before Angel stepped through the kitchen carrying a tray laden with food.

Savannah dropped her face in her hands. "My poor Whinny."

"A gray roan?"

She raised her head. Her eyes shined as her voice wavered with hope. "You found her?"

Brennan caught himself smiling. The clues fell together. The long hair. The well-groomed mare. "She's healing up fine behind the jail—" Before he could finish, Miss Louis flung her arms around his neck in obvious joy.

A clang of dishes smashed against the floor. Brennan turned as he made to pull the young woman's arms off his neck. Angel stood open mouthed, the empty tray dangling in her hand.

Chapter Six

Brennan finished the interrogation and returned to the jail. He paced the office and waited for Colton to serve the prisoners their morning meal of oatmeal and biscuits.

Once more, Brennan seemed to have upset the pretty, blonde waitress. Why had guilt settled over him like a rain cloud as soon as he met Angel's gaze? He hadn't done anything wrong. In fact, he wasn't the one who'd done the hugging. Savannah had, or uh, Miss Louis. He swiped his brow. That was a mistake he didn't want to make in front of Angel. Not that it should matter. They weren't courting. Nor had he given the subject any thought.

Then why did her feelings matter so much?

He cast the foolish question aside as Colton returned. "Why weren't you with Angel this morning?" His deputy barely had a foot in the room when Brennan tossed out the question. Although it was unusual for him to inquire about Colton's sisters, the morning's excitement still haunted his thoughts.

Colton raised an eyebrow, but waited until he'd closed the door to comment. "I had a lot on my mind yesterday and overslept, which I blame Angel and Emma for not waking me."

Brennan ran a hand through his hair and informed Colton of the incident with his sister and the coach.

"Thank God she's okay. If you hadn't—"

"Don't go there." Brennan struggled with the same nagging thought. "I caught up with Thad and the young lady he was transporting. Her name's Savannah Louis. Know any Louis's?"

Colton shook his head, still appearing dazed from the former news.

"She says she'd been helping an aunt north of Lincoln and was headed back home to St. Genevieve." He leaned back and scrubbed his hand across his jaw. "She came across an old satchel hidden near the river."

Colton leaned forward. "What was in it?"

"Cash."

"Enough to fill a couple of banks?"

"Not from the sound of things. She did mention some papers, but got scared before she had a chance to read them."

"Can't read, huh?"

"Said she could." Brennan drummed the ends of his fingers against the top of his scarred desk. "She flagged Thad on his return route the next morning. That would've given her plenty of time to read them."

"Where is she now?"

"I've got her working for the Meyers. Your sister could use the relief."

"Do you think she'll run?"

"No. She hasn't a penny to her name. Plus, she loves her mare too much to leave her. She's definitely here until the horse heals." He read over the facts he'd jotted down. "The men who robbed the coach had their faces covered. Thad said it all happened fairly quick once they were stopped. Two gunmen on either side of the coach held up him and Miss Louis while another man he couldn't see grabbed the satchel."

"That hardly makes sense. They didn't take anything else or threaten the passenger?"

Brennan shook his head. "Appears they knew what they were after and didn't have time to waste with added trouble."

The morning had only proven to add up loose ends. Brennan needed a change of topic. "Find anything yesterday?"

Colton remained quiet until firmly seated behind his desk. His eyes narrowed in disgust. "I don't know your opinion of this fancy Lincoln deputy, but I think he's as worthless as a four-legged snake," his voice lowered, "and maybe as dangerous."

Brennan cocked his head to the side. Harris, dangerous? Spurs jingled outside on the boardwalk as he waited for Colton to divulge more. The door swung open emitting the very serpent they spoke of.

"Morning, gents." Harris hung one hand over the top of the open door and saddled the other on his hip. The room tensed with his sudden appearance.

He turned his attention to Colton as a curious expression crept across his face. "Deputy, your sister," Harris's smile took on a mocking glint as he pivoted from Colton and peered across the street, "has a silly mind about courting and marrying."

From his desk chair, Colton dropped his pencil and slowly turned. "What do you know about Angel?"

"You'll remember I was good enough to keep her company last night." A taunting whine laced his words.

Brennan tensed. Without realizing his actions, he ground his teeth, and the palm of his hand grazed the handle of his pistol. What form of company did Harris refer to? If not for Colton's presence, he'd take the matter into his own hands. As it was, he forced himself to stand aside.

"And that's all you'll learn about her." Colton grabbed his hat from off the wall behind him. "Isn't there some place you're supposed to be?" He added with a mutter, "Like Lincoln."

"Harris," Brennan brushed past him onto the boardwalk. "I want to know if any of the locals have seen the men from the robberies. Ask around and report back. Colton, come with me."

Brennan didn't check how Harris received the order. He had more important matters to tend. He slammed the door to the jail then he and Colton mounted their horses. First order of business—wire Sheriff Douglas.

Brennan reined his horse to a halt outside the telegraph office. "Did you and Harris find any leads yesterday or not?"

"Harris?" Colton adjusted his hat over his hardened face. "That oily—he took off on a rabbit trail, supposedly so we'd search two areas. I spent an extra hour just looking for him before heading back."

He swung open the door. "The only thing I found was how worthless he is!"

Brennan paused in the doorway. If Harris wasn't with Colton, could he have doubled backed to the river?

"Morning, Sheriff." Robert nodded toward Colton. "Deputy."

"I know it's too early to expect Lincoln to have anything up and running, but I want you to try sending a wire every day 'til you get through." Brennan stared out the window. "Tell Sheriff Douglas we need to meet."

"Sure thing." Robert's past with an outlaw for an adopted father made him all business when it came to matters of the law.

Brennan pivoted to the door then stalled. "Has Deputy Harris been by?"

"Not that I know of. What's the man look like?"

"He's all teeth and fancy cloths." Colton answered.

If Harris was in on the robberies, he had to know his time was short before someone caught on. That could only mean the next hit would have to happen fast. But would this morning's adventure change their plans? Assuming Harris and the other two gunmen had held up the coach, the realization they'd almost lost something important would surely be cause for rethinking their plans.

Brennan scratched his open palm. "Thanks Robert. Keep me informed if anyone new stops in."

Colton followed him outside. "What's on your mind?"

"I caught three men cooling off at the river yesterday. If Harris returned shortly after taking the other route, he might have been one of them."

Colton kicked at a stone, spooking his horse. "Send the snake back. He's nothing but trouble."

"We can't send him back. If he's behind the thefts we can play him into our hands."

Before they rode out of town to follow up on a report of cattle rustling and to check the cave Savannah had mentioned Brennan and Colton stopped in at Hall's grocery store.

Brennan's Aunt Kate turned from straightening items on a shelf and smiled. "Good morning, boys. Need something for the trail?"

Brennan removed his hat and selected a couple of red apples. "Actually, we stopped by to see if—"

"Hi, Grandma! Daddy said I could help you out today while he's at the telegrapher's office and Mama visits her friend Sara."

Aunt Kate bent to hug her grandson. The boy had grown a full head since coming to Warsaw with Robert. "Of course you can. You're always a big help, but wait to get started until after Brennan finishes what he was saying."

"Oh, sorry, Sheriff."

"That's all right." Brennan tossed him one of the apples he'd chosen. "Have you had any new faces in the store?"

Aunt Kate raised her brows. "Ruthie made mention of two new customers. One was the tallest man she'd ever witnessed, while the other one was slight. She said he reminded her of a weasel—"

Her hands flew to her mouth. "Oh, I shouldn't repeat that."

"Don't hold back on my account. You know little details can often make or break a case."

Ruthie, Aunt Kate's youngest daughter, moved from behind the counter. "I'd be happy to tell you what I thought about him. Because I also caught him stealing fruit on the way out of the store."

"Why didn't you report it to us?" Colton asked.

"Honestly, I was just glad to see them gone. The weasel-like one had small beady eyes and a long nose. He was rather jumpy."

Colton spoke in a hushed tone to Brennan. "Sounds like the same description of our pickpocket."

Brennan chose another apple. "What did they purchase?"

"Just staples and in small amounts. They weren't stocking cupboards."

Brennan thanked them for the information and paid for the fruit. Outside, he tossed an apple to Colton then headed out of town. "Sounds like the bank's in danger for sure."

Colton finished chewing a large bite of the ripe fruit, then asked, "Where do you think they're hiding out?"

Brennan ground his teeth. "Right under our noses."

After riding a couple of miles in silence, Colton voiced his thoughts. "I don't like Harris's interest in Angel." Colton readjusted his hat. The horses had slowed as they neared the next farm. "Of course, maybe since he's heard of her silly dreams he'll back off."

"Dreams?" Something inside Brennan warned him not to ask, but curiosity wouldn't leave the subject alone.

"Angel's dreamt of her future husband for the last two years." Colton sighed and swiped a hand down his face. "She's determined to marry him only she's never seen his face."

Brennan moved in his saddle, suddenly uncomfortable. This meant Colton hadn't misled Harris. In Angel's mind, she was spoken for. "Then how does she know who he is?"

"In her dreams, he keeps saving her."

A sudden weight settled in Brennan's gut with the intensity of a steel ball. "Has anyone else saved her?"

"What do you mean—" For a moment Colton stared at Brennan before his eyes lit with a smug intelligence. "This morning and the stage coach."

Brennan wasn't sure how to receive the news. Why would she put stock in a dream? His breathing became shallow. Did she think he was the one? It would explain why she was upset over Miss Louis clinging to his neck.

But what it failed to explain was *his* reaction to Angel. Why he couldn't stand to upset her, why he flinched every time a man showed her attention … and why he'd bought the rocking chairs Angel admired most.

Colton cleared his throat and broke the prolonged silence. "Angel would be a lot safer if she was courted. She's refused every one that's offered, but she might not if—"

"No." Brennan cut him off before Colton could finish his outspoken thought. The idea was preposterous. Angel was too … well, she was too … what was she? Pretty and sweet. Innocent, naïve. Devoted and … lovely.

"Angel needs more protection than I can offer." Colton clicked his tongue to pick up speed. "She'd be safer keeping house, not waiting tables. If you're not interested, I'll find someone who is."

The reins pinched Brennan's palms from where he wrung them in his hands. Denial was fruitless … he couldn't have another man courting Angel. A fact Colton was well aware of.

***

Angel massaged her sore calf muscles as she sat on the back step of the restaurant. *Thank you, Lord, for sending help. But don't let—*

She stalled and considered how to word her prayer. God already knew her heart, but admitting jealousy was a hard truth to face. *Okay, you know what I'm feeling. But in defense, Brennan did save me today.*

Her dreams pushed to the surface. Brennan's physique fit the images of the elusive man. A strong urge to list the reasons why the sheriff should be hers and not Savannah's tempted her thoughts. But excuses couldn't prolong the inevitable. God would see His will was done. And regardless of that decision, Angel had to accept He knew what was best.

She sighed heavily. If only her mind wouldn't worry over what decision He made.

Angel slid back inside and studied the kitchen scene. Breakfast had passed leaving a lull until lunch time. Savannah, brightened after eating breakfast, took to the dishes as if she'd been starved for work. Like with the stray cat, Angel's heart softened toward the girl.

Although there were still tables to set, they could use a few more minutes of rest. "Savannah, why don't you step outside with me?"

A wave of hair swayed in the air as Savannah turned toward the sound of Angel's voice. She faced the cook who gave a nod of approval.

Angel ran a hand down the length of Savannah's red strands. "How do you get it to grow so long?"

She shrugged. "Mama's is long, too."

Curious about her past, Angel pressed for more information. "Is that where you were headed? Back home?"

"Yep. Aunt Sadie healed up good after her fall and didn't need me no more."

The girl's English could use a lot of improvement. Maybe she'd stay long enough Angel and Emma could give her lessons. She eyed Savannah's hair again. The patrons would accuse them of having a horse in the kitchen if a strand of that length made its way onto a plate. "Why don't I braid your hair, so it won't get messy in the kitchen?"

"The Bible says not to pleat your hair. Mama says it's a sinful practice."

Angel patted the braided bun she'd quickly piled at the back of her head that morning. She'd never considered any of her hair styles as sinful, but she had heard of folks with strict practices.

Savannah's dress was a simple frock of gray. Did she not wear anything of color either? Angel eyed the blue calico she'd donned that morning, peeking out around her apron. She loved to absorb the colors of God's creation. Whether in the sky, on the land, or dyed in many types of fabrics, she didn't view it as wrong, but as a gift to use.

Her thoughts returned to Savannah and her hair. "I don't think that's what Paul meant when he spoke about braids. I think he was speaking about the jewelry women of that time who wove in their hair."

She held the girl's rapt attention. Something inside Savannah seemed to long for a better explanation. Angel could understand why. With hair that long, a braid would help keep it under control.

Angel continued, "It's one thing to draw the wrong type of attention and quite another to do something for ease of your circumstances. In a kitchen, we need to insure our hair won't be served to our customers."

A crease formed in Savannah's forehead as she lifted her hair in her hand. "And God sees my heart, so He'll know I'm not doing it for sinful reasons."

Angel smiled and began overlapping one thick handful over another. Soft and shiny, it was evident Savannah took pride in the lovely gift God had given her.

"Sheriff Brennan shore is nice. Han'som, too."

Angel's hands stiffened. "Yes, he is."

"Is he married?"

Angel jerked at the question.

"Ow! Be easy."

"Sorry." Angel bit her lip, her heart hammered against her chest. She'd like nothing better than to say the sheriff was spoken for. But she couldn't lie. An unspoken prayer trembled across her lips.

The stray cat emerged from beneath the steps and weaved against Savannah's legs. "Oh, I love cats."

Angel was able to breathe again, thankful for the change of subject. Since when had she become so possessive of Sheriff Brennan?

A smile lit inside and warmed her cheeks. She could still feel the quick beat of his heart as Brennan held her against him. Had he felt the same tremor when their hands touched? Did he think of her now?

"You never answered my question." Savannah stared back at Angel as she stroked the cat's head. "Is he married?"

The earlier warmth Angel felt hardened to a block of ice. What would it take to distract this persistent stranger?

Chapter Seven

The day drew to a close too quickly for Angel. Although nervous to know how the sheriff would react again to Savannah, Angel had anticipated seeing Brennan at lunch, only he and Colton never stopped in.

Savannah crossed her line of vision, her long, thick braid cascading down her back. It was just as well he didn't show. The Meyers' were still cross with Angel for breaking the dishes. She couldn't risk dropping more.

Colton appeared at the back door. "Sis, I'll wait for you out here." His eyes trailed to Savannah as she returned from cleaning off the last table.

Angel watched as they beheld one another. Savannah turned a light shade of pink as Colton's eyes trailed the length of her braid. As if suddenly feeling ashamed, Savannah turned and ran back into the diner.

"Colton, you shouldn't have stared at her like that. This is the first time she's ever worn a braid. She'll probably never want to do it again."

Colton shook his head and raised his hands palms up. "I didn't do anything ... but she sure is a pretty thing."

"Sshhh. She'll never want to come home with me if you talk like that."

"Come home with you?" Mrs. Meyer stopped beside them. "Not with an unmarried man in the house. Wouldn't be proper. The girl will stay with us."

"Right?" She waited for her husband's confirmation.

Mr. Meyer nodded in agreement, but as usual, had very little to say.

Angel swallowed in relief. She could go home and rest without worrying when the next question would emerge about the sheriff. Savannah hadn't let the topic drop. Although … now that she'd met Colton, would her interest wane? An idea formed. Angel wasn't a matchmaker, but she knew of one in town. Maybe a little hint dropped here and there would do the trick. Even as she toyed with the idea, her conscience reminded her to leave it with God.

But would she?

***

Halfway home, Angel pivoted on the hard wagon bench toward her brother. "Why didn't you and Sheriff Brennan stop in to eat today?" The question had been burning too long.

"Busy working." He stared at her for an awkward length of time.

What was he thinking? Had Sheriff Brennan asked about her? A girl could hope.

"Angel, it's time you considered settling down."

She stopped breathing. Her heart paused between beats and twirled inside her chest. Angel unconsciously primped by pushing stray strands of hair behind her ear. She cleared her throat and tried to retain a look of controlled interest. "Has someone asked about me?"

A muscle bulged on the side of her brother's jaw. "Brennan told me what happened this morning with you and the coach."

"Yes ..." the word dragged from her throat. Angel waited for Colton's lips to mouth the news she longed to hear, but his features only hardened.

Her brother knew of her dreams. Why would he ... her chest tightened as panic hurled possible scenarios through her mind. Had Colton proposed to someone? Did he want the family homestead to himself and his forthcoming wife? Not only did she not have a place to go, but that would also mean there wouldn't be a chance of him pursuing Savannah.

Angel's shoulders sagged as she watched the last remnants of pink and purple settle in the horizon. The girl would continue to seek Brennan's attention.

She dreaded her brother's reasoning, but finally asked the inevitable, "What does that have to do with my marrying?"

"I can't always be there to look after you." He rubbed a palm over his knee. Of course Colton hadn't proposed to anyone. He was driven by his concern of losing her like they had their parents.

Her remaining fog of optimism faded leaving a painful reality. Brennan hadn't asked to court her. She blinked back a mound of disappointment and gripped her skirt, wrinkling the fabric.

"If he hadn't been there—" Her brother's hands tightened around the reins.

Angel quieted Colton's nerves with a gentle hand on his arm. "But he was there. Just like in my dream. And he'll be there the other times, too."

"Other times? How many times are you going to get run over?"

Angel smiled at his endless worry. "Not every scenario is the same." Her throat constricted and her smile faded with the haunting image of the stampede. She cleared her throat and sought for a strength she didn't feel for the sake of her brother. "The sheriff will be there. He won't let me get hurt."

"How do you know it's him?"

"He saved me today, didn't he?" Even as she said the words, doubt clouded her reasoning. What if it wasn't Sheriff Brennan?

She didn't want it to be someone else. Although she wasn't sure when it happened, she'd developed feelings toward the lawman. Always before, she'd viewed him as the man who'd once tried to court her best friend, Juliann. But that time had passed. Julie had married Robert.

And then of course, there was the business with Sara Douglas. But that had been a nasty joke by men intent on getting even with Brennan.

Poor Sara, coming to Warsaw as a mail-order bride, only to find she didn't have a realistic fiancé. In God's goodness though, He saw fit to provide for her—with Brennan's cousin, the lawyer.

Angel chuckled.

"What's so funny?"

Angel widened her eyes, unaware she'd made a sound. "Oh, I was just thinking of the sheriff's past. His experiences with courting haven't ended very favorably, have they?" A familiar thought entered her mind. Would he ever consider courting again? She worried her lip.

Colton's face hardened. "Don't build false hopes, Angela."

Her brother rarely used her full name. The fact he did now couldn't be good.

But what am I supposed to think, God? In the Bible, You spoke to servants, kings, and Your disciples in visions and dreams. I don't believe You've changed. You're still the same today as You were yesterday. Why can't others accept You've spoken to me this way?

The reason came softly. She could almost hear Sarah laughing as Abraham told her she would be a mother in her old age; Joseph's brothers loud mocking for thinking they would one day bow down to him; and Eli growing weary with Samuel for repeatedly waking him.

Though different in circumstance, like her, they faced disbelief, too.

"Angel, have you heard a word I've said?" Colton pulled back on the reins as they neared their barn.

Angel jerked her attention from her thoughts. "I'm sorry. I guess not."

He sighed. "I talked to Clara. We both agree Cecil would make a sound husband—"

"I can't marry Cecil!" Her heart beat faster and plummeted in the same instant. "He's not the one."

Even as she defended her position, she understood how hard it was for others to accept.

God, help me out. Don't let them force me away from Your will.

Angel leapt from the wagon before it stopped. She stumbled to find her balance then rushed past the house to an old maple tree. She buried her arms and face against the tree's broad trunk as almond sized tears tumbled from her eyes.

She couldn't deal with this. Not after the toil of today. *I'm sorry for being this way, Lord. I don't like it, but I can't seem to make it stop.* Her air exhaled in short bursts as more emotion sought release. *Take away my hurt. Please, step in and save me.*

Moments later, her emotions spent, Angel rolled her shoulders over the rough bark and collapsed against the tree. Dusk had vanished leaving a blanket of stars spread across an inky black and blue sky. Between deep breaths, she peered through the canopy of leaves to the twinkling firmament.

As she tried to change focus, her thoughts returned to Savannah.

Something had to be done about the girl's misguided feelings. Brennan hadn't caught the men who'd held up the stage nor had he saved her from danger.

He was *Angel's* rescuer.

An owl's hoot questioned her thought.

He is mine. Isn't he, God?

Thaddeus had been the one with Savannah. If she wanted to build a crush, she should build it on him.

Humor pulled at her lips despite her tumultuous mood. Thaddeus wasn't exactly the kind of man that caused a woman to pine away. A knotty branch when compared to the solid oak of Brennan.

Angel sighed. *Why can't I leave my worry with You, God?*

***

The next morning didn't improve Angel's mood. She arrived at the diner behind Savannah who had walked over with the Meyers. Savannah grabbed the first apron off the wall—the one Angel always wore—then commenced to cracking eggs as if she'd worked here every day of her life.

A knot of self-pity hardened Angel's stomach and weakened her limbs. Neither Mr. nor Mrs. Meyer had greeted her. Their attention remained riveted on their "adopted daughter." More like a passing thief for all Angel's identity she was stealing.

Nearly four years she'd given the Meyers. Working without complaint when they were short on help. Carrying both duties of a waitress and assistant cook when one was sick.

And now, because of a temporary house guest, they couldn't acknowledge her?

Angel's eyes stung. Clara's barbs she could take. Folks thinking she wasn't a deep thinker she'd accepted. But after years of service to be ignored because of someone with eyes for—

The room became still. Angel's eyes trailed from the peeler in her hands, past the waste bucket, to the potato peelings pointing a haphazard line at her shocked employers and their prized protégé.

Her throat constricted as she stared from one to another.

Her job supported her dream home. She couldn't lose her employment. If she lost the sheriff to Savannah, she at least wanted the house. "Sorry. I'll clean this up."

"What are you doing peeling potatoes anyway?" Mrs. Meyers grabbed the vegetable shredder from a side bin and snatched the potato from Angel's hand. "We serve hash-browns for breakfast, hon'."

A lump formed in her throat. "I'll ready the dining room." She left in a hurried pace amid chuckles from her employers. She almost wished they were mad rather than humored. Couldn't they see her turmoil? Didn't they care?

Alone, Angel released a long breath and tried to quiet her internal chaos. The Meyers hadn't been upset, but how long would their patience remain if she continued to make mistakes?

"I bet I know why folks call you Angel." Savannah appeared and removed half the stack of plates from Angel's arms and began setting the tables. "It's because you're so sweet."

Angel's shoulders slumped. *Why was it so much trouble to dislike one little person?*

"The Meyers talked a lot last night. They're very proud of you." She tossed her braid behind her. "I ain't never worked at a restaurant before, so I want to do my best to make 'em proud of me, too."

Angel forced a smile and swallowed hard. Her feelings hadn't been right ... but they had been justified. She'd do better, try harder. After all,

Savannah did work hard. She was pleasant. And she—

"When do you think the sheriff'll be in?"

Angel paused over the table, a plate held in both hands. Her body turned rigid as though splashed with water fresh from the spring. She stared at the dinnerware and fought off a building desire to smash it against the floor, then raised her head. After a deep breath she replied in her usual calm voice, "Lunch time, along with a lot of *other* men."

Her break couldn't come fast enough. Finally, two hours after the breakfast crowd, Angel freed herself from the diner and stared through the jewelry store's window. Trinkets of gold and silver, along with several colorful gems, shimmered in the sunlight enough to cause any woman to covet.

Had Mr. Davis bought Emma's ring here or had he ordered it? Her sister's princess cut diamond, though small, shone like the nighttime stars from last evening. A sigh escaped her. Would her turn ever come? Some days were harder than others to stay faithful to a dream.

She turned away knowing nothing good could come from wishing. Time to return to the diner and … Savannah—the very reason she'd spent her break walking the boardwalk rather than on the back stoop.

Several hours passed in a painfully slow procession as Savannah, in her eagerness to please the Meyers, tried to take over and outdo the senior waitress's responsibilities.

"Oh, look, the sheriff's here." Savannah rushed out to Angel's table.

Angel grabbed at the strings of her frayed, stained apron and fumbled to retie them. "Err! That girl might find her braid nailed to the floor one day."

***

Brennan scratched his chin and shifted uncomfortably. The other patrons hadn't seemed to notice the rapt attention lavished on him by Miss Louis. *Good.* The young woman acted enamored for some unexplainable reason. Brennan rubbed the back of his neck and tried to shake his reaction, which felt close to a bee hive in a bear's den.

The questions she had about her horse, Whinny, were the same as she'd asked yesterday evening when he'd checked in with the Meyers. Her silly antics were those of a school girl more than an adult. Maybe she was younger than he first assumed. Either way, he was ready for Whinny to be well enough to load on a train for them both to go home.

He glanced toward the kitchen. Why hadn't Angel taken his order? Her presence had become expected. He craned an ear toward the back but couldn't hear anything over the noise of the establishment. Frustrated he contemplated entering the kitchen to make sure she was there when Angel breezed into the diner.

Without his approval, Brennan's heart pattered in his chest. He cleared his throat but couldn't quite pull his eyes away. How had it come to this? In a matter of milliseconds, he'd worried if Angel was all right, if she was mad, or worse, if she'd accepted another's proposal and quit work. He smiled at his foolishness.

"You're happy today." Angel's voice faltered, her eyes dropped from his.

Air rushed into his lungs. "Just glad to see I didn't lose you to the other gal."

Angel's head popped back up as familiar dimples formed on either side of her smile. "Oh, and why's that?"

He narrowed his eyes and peered at her delicate face. If she was fishing for his feelings, she expected too much. Brennan didn't yet know how to deal with them himself. If he wasn't careful, he'd make a mess of it all, and like with Julie and Sarah, lose out again. He avoided a direct answer and replied, "I've got to make sure these cowpokes don't give you too much trouble."

Her halted nod was enough to realize his reply hadn't been enough. Brennan squared his jaw. If Angel meant anything to him at all, he should take the risk.

Indecision marred his thinking. Was he ready to take that step? He'd chew on the thought over his meal. There was plenty of time.

Chapter Eight

"Come on, sleepy-head, wake up. You're going to make us late."

A blurry version of Emma came into Angel's view. Her wedding! Angel shot of bed. "Oh, you can't be late. I'll get your veil."

"My veil?" Emma cocked her head and raised an eyebrow.

Angel eyed Emma's yellow cotton dress.

It was Sunday.

"Oh." She took a step back and bumped against her mattress. Plopping onto the edge of the bed, she ran her fingers through her hair, combing it back from her face. "I was dreaming it was your wedding day."

"That's not for another week." Emma opened Angel's wardrobe and removed a dress. "I thought I woke you up the first time. You must have been sleeping really hard."

Emma draped the dress over her arm. "Are you okay? You didn't sleep well, did you?"

Angel rubbed her eyes and shook her head in agreement.

"Was it that scary dream from the other night? The one you won't tell me about?"

Knowing Emma, like Colton, would only fret if she knew the dream of the stampede, Angel had chosen to keep it to herself. But last night hadn't been dreams of danger and her rescuer, at least not in the usual sense. Instead, she'd dreamed of Savannah … and Brennan.

"No, it wasn't about that." She stood and wavered.

Emma offered her arm. "You jumped out of bed too fast. *Tsk, tsk*. You'll be fighting dizzies all day."

Emma was right. Half an hour later Angel stood for the opening hymn and grasped the front pew as the room swayed. She focused on the cross overhanging the pulpit and took a deep breath. The preaching had yet to start and already she anticipated lunch. In a hurry, she'd only eaten a piece of bread for breakfast. Looking back, she should've grabbed the last two slices of bacon Emma had fried.

Movement a few rows over revealed Savannah, standing next to the Meyers, sweeping her gaze over the room. Angel resisted the urge to do likewise. If Sheriff Brennan were here, surely Savannah would have spotted him by now. Angel licked her lips, straining to keep from glancing to Brennan's usual seat.

Savannah's dark brown eyes swept toward the front and paused for the briefest moment on Colton. Immersed in song, he hadn't noticed. Angel peered at the new waitress again. A soft pink glow brightened her cheeks. Hmm … maybe she had less to worry about than she'd first assumed. Or maybe Savannah was just trouble all the way around.

After the opening prayer, the pastor read scripture from Galatians chapter five, listing manifested works of the flesh. "If you're here today and you fall under any of these, *why* are you suffering?" He didn't wait for an answer, but continued, "In short, you've turned from trusting Jesus Christ to satisfy you and instead placed your trust in the world.

"You say, 'Pastor, how can I stop sin's desires?' Set your eyes back on Jesus. Next, accept you can't overcome the sin in your current state. So the first step you must take is to trust Him to forgive you and change you. He can and will deliver you."

Angel reread the scripture. Did she suffer from any of the sins listed? Slowly, she brought her head up to peep at Savannah. Guilt descended over her heart. Jealousy was a close kin to envy. *God, I'm sorry. I didn't know where this was going, but I've definitely fallen into jealousy. And over a man that isn't even mine!* She returned her attention to the message.

"Be patient," the pastor was saying. "And pray earnestly until you experience the Spirit changing your heart.

"Never stop pouring out your longing to your heavenly Father. As written in Psalms, 'let your soul thirst after God.' God promises He won't withhold good from you. Believe this and experience spiritual renewal."

As the sermon neared its close, Angel again caught Savannah peeking over her shoulder. This time the girl didn't strain far as her curiosity seemed centered on Colton.

Mrs. Meyer glimpsed from her new charge to the subject of interest. A crinkle formed at the corner of her eye and a look of general approval softened her features.

After the service ended, Angel made small talk with several of the congregation as she followed Colton outside. As Emma's Sundays were often spent with the Davis family, she had already said good-bye. Now she and Todd stood talking to Julie and Robert.

Mrs. Meyer stopped beside Colton. "I have a ham in the oven. Why don't you come over and enjoy it with us?" She winked at Angel but didn't share the invite.

Angel swallowed back instant rejection. She tightened her hands around her Bible. *Don't envy. Don't be jealous.*

Savannah, standing on the other side of the cook, shifted her weight. The movement grabbed Angel's attention. Again, a soft color heightened the girl's cheeks. Maybe being left out could be a good thing.

"I'd be glad to. Err ..." he glimpsed at Angel, as if wondering if the invitation was extended to her, too.

"Angel," Cecil moved through the crowd of people that still visited outside the church. "Clara invited us for dinner." He swatted his hat against his leg. "I'd like it if you'd allow me to escort you."

This was news to her. Clara hadn't said a word earlier in the week. Of course, their conversation including Cecil hadn't been agreeable. She considered a polite way to decline without offending Cecil. "Thank you, but—"

Colton ruined her escape. "That's great. Now we all have a place to be. See you later this afternoon, Sis."

Angel's gaze fell to the ground. It was better for the dirt to witness her disappointment than poor Cecil. The man had a good nature and a nice appearance, even handsome, but his heart didn't cause hers to beat wildly like Brennan's.

Cecil held out his arm. "I brought the wagon."

Angel fell into step beside him. The fact he hadn't ridden his horse was evidence the invite hadn't been on a whim. Clara had planned the afternoon. Oh, her siblings!

"Clara's made a pork roast with all the fixings."

Angel tried to return Cecil's smile, but her heavy heart pulled at her mouth, making even a half-grin difficult. Where was the sheriff? Perhaps seeing him would lighten her mood.

"Cecil," Clara's father-in-law called his son over.

"Excuse me. I'll learn what Father needs before we go." Cecil left Angel standing alone.

She maneuvered to the edge of the church yard to stand out of the way of moving wagons and watched the families trail toward their destinations.

"Are you eating at your sister's house today?"

Angel raised her eyes and met Sheriff Brennan's. Like spring-time blooming in her heart, her mood freshened at his presence. "I guess so. It was news to me."

He nodded and held her attention. If he wanted to know more, all he had to do was ask. She wouldn't withhold anything from him.

His eyes dropped to the ground beside her as his hand went to his belt. "Don't move, Angel."

Fully trusting in the man, Angel did as asked. She froze not only her limbs but also her thoughts, not wanting to imagine what alarmed the sheriff. But she couldn't ignore the rustle in the leaves. Nor the hiss and rattle.

"Brennan," she squeaked, "what do I do?"

His hand stayed on his holster instead of withdrawing his pistol. Angel pictured the stump beside her. She stood too close to the snake. And with the added fullness of her skirt, the sheriff didn't have a clear shot.

"Stay where you are. Keep focusing ahead." His strong voice remained calm, caressing her fear to a controllable level.

Brennan took three full strides and positioned himself to the side and behind her. The snake's rattle grew more intense. Angel's predicament caught the attention of several remaining congregation members, including Cecil. His worried eyes turned toward her as voices fell to a hush.

Angel turned her head and chanced a peek. Her skirt swayed to the side revealing the diamond shaped head of the coiled rattlesnake. A cold sweat broke out on top of her skin as her breathing came in short gasps. Angel could almost feel the pain of the snake's poisonous fangs sinking into her leg.

"Be still, sweetheart." Brennan's confident tone rallied her courage. He placed a firm hand on her arm sending a surge of warmth through her frozen limb. At the same time he shoved her to the side, his raised boot crashed down on the serpent's head.

Angel would have fallen save for Brennan's tight grasp. He pulled her back as he finished twisting the heel of his boot against the uneven stump. She shuddered and felt her body lighten as a wave of nausea overtook her.

The next moment, Angel found herself in Brennan's capable arms. The raised voices of men livened her senses.

"She has no business going anywhere but home, and I intend to take her there." Brennan's grip around her tightened.

"Sheriff, with all due respect, I brought my wagon. She'll be fine and her sister can see to her." Cecil argued his position.

Angel raised her head then let it roll to the side against Brennan's shoulder. Rising too quickly from bed this morning, coupled with the shock of nearly being bitten sapped her of strength. But if she wanted Brennan to win his argument, she'd have to summon enough energy to at least stand on her feet.

Angel took a deep breath and moved enough Brennan released her. "I think it's best if I went home, Cecil."

Cecil squared his jaw and peered from her to Brennan, whose arm she still clung to for partial support. He seemed to search for an acceptable outcome.

Without waiting for his response, Brennan led her the few feet to his horse and lifted her onto the saddle.

The rush of movement sent a flash of stars to her eyes. She grasped the saddle horn to keep from falling. A wagon ride home would be the sensible solution followed by an afternoon of rest, but Brennan didn't have a wagon.

She took a deep breath and slowly released it. "Cecil, don't miss out on Clara's dinner. No one cooks a pork roast as good as she does."

His forehead wrinkled with a frown, but before he could object, she proposed a solution. "Maybe I can join one with you next time."

His features relaxed as he shook his head in acceptance. "If that's the way you want it. Next time then." He turned his attention to Brennan and scowled before walking away.

***

Brennan led Buck down the road and kept pace beside the saddle. His mind replayed the church scene, repeating Angel's sweet voice calling him by name rather than sheriff. That was a sound he could get used to.

"You okay, up there? You're still a little pale."

Angel smiled sweetly from on top of Buck. "I'm fine, thank you."

He stared a moment longer. "Sorry you'll miss out on your sister's cooking." He wasn't really. Brennan didn't like the idea of Cecil trying to court Angel. And when he saw them walking toward Cecil's wagon, his whole world had come to a stop. Obviously, time wasn't as generous as he'd thought.

"They'll be other dinners."

Brennan mulled over her comment and the one she'd made to Clara's brother-in-law. Did she want to spend time with Cecil? He struggled to accept the possibility. Not that Brennan had anything against him personally, but Cecil wasn't good enough for her. Angel deserved someone who could give her more than a hard life on a farm.

He saw her in his mind, walking down the boardwalk, gazing through shop windows and talking to those she passed by. "If you could choose, would you stay in the country or live in town?"

"Town, definitely." She answered without hesitation.

See Cecil, you can't give her what she wants.

"I enjoy all the sights and sounds. The colorful shops and houses, and the people. How about you?"

"Same. Well, maybe not the colorful shops." He returned her giggle with a smile. "Would you still choose my house or is there another one you like as well?"

"Yours. You know it will break my heart if it sells before I save enough—"

"You're saving to buy my house?" Brennan's curiosity piqued.

She pulled a shoulder upward. "I know it's unusual…"

"Like your dreams?"

Angel's eyes widened as her mouth dropped open. "How do you know about them? Did Colton tell you?"

Brennan pulled Buck to a halt and leaned an arm over his neck. "If he hadn't of, Harris would've made sure I knew."

"Ugh." Angel dropped her head. "That was a mistake."

Brennan didn't want to leave her feeling ashamed. He was kind of glad she'd told him. At least it led to him finding out. "Then I guess I'm two for two so far."

She met his eyes and a dimple appeared in her cheek. "The snake. You've now saved me twice."

The sun glinted off her light blonde hair. Waves of curls escaped her bun and now tickled her temples. Brennan had a strong desire to pull her from the horse and kiss her, but the idea was choked out by an earlier thought.

Unable to let it go, he finally asked, "What about Cecil. Where does he fit in?" He held his breath waiting for an answer, but it was slow to come.

Angel focused over the top of Buck's head and expelled a breath of air. "You'd have to ask Clara and Colton about that one." With a sad expression, she shook her head as though unwilling to voice the rest of her thoughts.

A nervous beat drummed in Brennan's chest. Angel didn't appear upset over missing out with Cecil. Did that mean Brennan might mean something to her? Did he encourage what was building between them? He risked rejection for sure. It happened every time. But if he didn't take the risk, he chanced losing her to Cecil or some other persistent man.

In a moment of confidence, he reached for her hand but never made contact. Angel gasped and pointed straight ahead. "An Indian!"

Chapter Nine

Brennan glimpsed past Angel to the road and paused on her reason for alarm … a lone Indian walking beside a horse. Brennan recognized the familiar gait long before their paths crossed. An acquaintance for years, he knew the Indian well.

"What do we do?" Angel's whispered worry proved she didn't.

"It's just Walking Tall." Although disappointed his opportunity with Angel had been interrupted, he'd half expected to meet up with the Osage. "Hope you're not in a hurry. He likes to trade."

Angel's eyes widened in wonder before a smile brightened her features. He loved watching her come aglow.

He felt in his pocket for what he might trade to give something for Angel to take home. Nothing but coins. In his vest pocket was a watch from his grandfather, but it wasn't something to part with.

"Sheriff Brennan Douglas," Walking Tall stopped a few feet away. His intelligent eyes level with Brennan's. He stared from him to Buck. His disapproval barely discernable through his tight, emotionless face. "Short flank. Not good for lawman if horse cannot run good distance."

He got all that from one look at Buck? The Indian was right, but Brennan didn't like the shame brought by his own obvious lack of horse expertise, especially in front of Angel. "Buck does the job."

Walking Tall's gaze bore through him. Brennan ground his teeth, knowing he couldn't hide the truth from the man.

"Walking Tall has horse for you. He will guide you on next journey." The Indian glanced upward then to the red and white horse at his side. "Great Spirit says you will need Condor."

Brennan furrowed his brow as remnants of a dream flickered through his mind. He tried to capture the memory but only felt a familiarity between the dream and Walking Tall's presence.

He considered the trade. His current horse had been on duty less than a year, and Brennan never felt satisfied with his performance. The job of sheriff carried a heavy responsibility. He needed a horse equal to the task. Brennan notched his chin. "Just a minute."

Angel's broad smile proved she was enjoying the strange interaction. He rummaged through the first saddlebag. His fingers found a jar of hardtack. That wouldn't do. Brennan shoved it aside and saw his binoculars. Not a chance. They were too valuable.

Leaving the bag open, Brennan left it for the other side, trailing his hand across Buck's rump. No doubt, Walking Tall expected to take the buckskin as part of the trade.

Condor, as the other horse had been called, flicked his head. The muscles in his neck rippled with energy. His back bare, it was easy to view his symmetric shape. Built for speed, chances were the painted mustang could run circles around Buck.

Brennan's fingers brushed against something soft. He pulled out a velvet pouch he'd forgotten about and his mind reeled back to two years earlier. After starting the house, he'd traded his best hat and pocketknife for the contents of the pouch. Typical to his personality, he thought he'd had everyone figured out. But not so with Juliann.

He stretched the velvet mouth open and poured a heart pendent into his palm secured to a dainty chain. Funny how something once tied to his heart could now evoke so little emotion.

Although he didn't look up, he felt Angel's curious gaze as he retraced his steps. He added the money in his pocket to the jewelry and held his open palm toward Walking Tall.

The Indian stared at him, refusing to acknowledge Brennan's offer.

"Of course, the horse, too." Brennan offered Buck's reins.

Walking Tall's stare moved to Angel then back to Brennan's palm. He withdrew the chain and let the gold charm dangle in the air. The sun glinted off the metal drawing a sigh of admiration from Angel. Walking Tall stretched toward her and demanded, "Hand."

Deep dimples formed in her cheeks as Angel did as commanded and the Indian looped the chain over her wrist.

When his attention returned to Brennan, he grunted and pointed to the knife fastened to the sheriff's gun belt.

Ah rats, not my four-inch skinner. Brennan shifted his weight. *Why couldn't you take the money?* He scrubbed a hand over his clean–shaven face, missing the feel of stubble. A long sigh rumbled from his chest. The Indian didn't budge. Anyone else would willingly barter, but not Walking Tall.

Brennan eyed both horses. No doubt Walking Tall was right. Buck didn't perform well under normal duties. And with the threat of a bank robbery, Brennan needed a dependable animal.

The coins returned to his pocket. He shook his head and momentarily closed his eyes. Out of all the knives he'd owned, this particular one held the sharpest blade.

He swallowed his regret. No use mourning. After all, he'd still have his boot knife. With a flick of his thumb he unfastened the holder and presented the knife to its new owner. Walking Tall's eyes shone with interest as he admired one of Brennan's few prized possessions.

Condor snorted and stomped his front hoof. Brennan studied the two equines. The deal had to be square. "You might as well have this, too." He undid his belt and slid off the leather knife holder.

A semblance of a smile played on the Indian's sun-beaten features while Brennan helped Angel down and moved his saddle and tack from Buck to Condor.

When the exchange was complete, Brennan stood with Angel at his side and watched the Indian and Buck trail into the distance. He wrestled whether to be aggravated—he glanced beside him—

or enjoy the sheer pleasure the bracelet brought Angel.

***

As they neared home, Angel said, "I like it when you trade with that Indian." A giggle, she couldn't stifle, slipped past her lips.

Brennan kept his attention focused ahead, but as Angel leaned forward to rub the new horse's neck, she saw the tuck of humor in the corner of his mouth.

He looped the reins over the hitching rail in front of her family's house then reached for her waist. His eyes fell on the charm as he helped her down. Angel brought her arm toward her and with her other hand, peered closer at the gold heart. A faint inscription of wild flowers had been etched on the front and back. She bit her lip. As much as she wanted to, she couldn't keep the jewelry. It hadn't been given by Brennan.

"Here," Angel moved to slip the necklace from her wrist.

Brennan covered her hand with his. "Keep it."

The warmth of his skin ignited a shock-way of sensations. She lifted her eyes and her heartbeat quickened. Brennan's steady gaze swept over her face and paused on her mouth. *Kiss me, kiss me*, her heart seemed to beat.

Her eyes began to burn the longer he waited. She wet her lips. Still, they remained untouched. He wasn't going to kiss her. Was he thinking of Savannah? *No. Don't let your thoughts go there.*

She wanted to tip forward. Press her lips to his. To know what it was like to experience love. This was love, wasn't it?

Brennan's throat visibly constricted before he took a step back. His focus trailed from her mouth back to her eyes. "I might have been selfish, not letting you take a wagon." He shuffled his feet, putting more distance between them. "Hope you can rest well now that you're home."

A lump lodged in her throat, preventing any response. She broke eye contact and fought the pain of an unreleased sigh.

"Angel?"

The tenderness in his voice made her stop with her hand on the yard gate. With a prayer for courage, Angel lifted her head. "Yes?"

Brennan returned to her side and released the latch. He held the gate open. "Be careful of any newcomers in town. Don't easily trust them."

She entered the yard, Brennan didn't follow. Her throat burned but there was nothing that could quench it, at least nothing Brennan was willing to offer. Well aware of his past, she shouldn't have allowed her hopes to rise.

Her fingers trailed the top of the gate. Brennan's hand caught hers and pulled the gate closed, drawing them together from either side.

He toyed with a wayward curl near the nape of her neck. "And don't trust your heart to Cecil."

Surprised, she inhaled sharply.

Brennan's eyes darkened as his hands wrapped around her arms and tilted her forward. Angel willingly followed his lead, her lips aching for the contact. Like a searing brand his mouth touched hers, igniting a flame deep inside her heart.

***

Angel sang as she flitted from room to room through the empty house. Glad for the chance to be alone, she replayed every moment with Brennan, soaking in the joy of the afternoon. No longer feeling weak, she cleaned the house from top to bottom.

She came to a stop at her parents' bedroom. Like always, the door was left ajar. Angel pushed it open and stepped inside. For the first time in months, a longing to curl up at her mother's feet and lay her head in her lap overwhelmed Angel. If only Mother were here to share her joy. And Father, too. He'd no doubt offer sound advice.

Angel sat down on the double-wedding ring quilt spread across their bed. "I know what you both would say." She fingered the lace trim of a pillow case.

"Father, you would bring up Brennan's abundant confidence with a bit of warning. Mother, you would remark on his noble character." Angel sighed. "And you both would be right. Then I would tell you so many other wonderful things about him you would gladly give your blessing."

"Angel," Colton's voice filtered through the house from the front door, "are you home?"

Angel grabbed her dust cloth and broom and pulled the door partially closed behind her. "Did you have a nice dinner?" Her own excitement kept hidden, she focused on learning more about her brother and Savannah.

"A fine time." His eyes gave away what his tongue withheld. He was definitely interested in the longhaired girl. "How about you?"

Angel gave a short description of the change in her afternoon plans, omitting Brennan's kiss. Colton listened without response. Did he realize this made the second time Brennan saved her?

"I almost forgot to tell you. Mrs. Meyer said you don't have to come in until the dinner hour. She figured you were due for some time off and said they could get along fine with Savannah." He left for the kitchen. "What do you think you'll do with your free morning?"

Angel didn't move. A turmoil of thoughts invaded her mind. Wasn't it enough for Savannah to try to steal Brennan's attention, did she also have to snatch Angel's job?

***

Angel pattered into the kitchen the next morning after sleeping in an extra hour. She picked up a glass and caught the shine of the locket around her wrist. A surge of warmth rushed to her face. She took a deep breath and slowly released it. How would she face him at the diner without thinking about their kiss?

She wouldn't be at the diner today, at least not until dinner. Which meant Savannah would wait his table. Angel filled her glass with water, biting her lip in irritation. She brought the drink to her mouth then paused.

Colton would also be at the table.

Satisfied with the small fact, she swallowed the cool liquid then stood over the stove interested in what Emma was cooking. Angel picked up a wooden spoon resting on top of a pan of boiling eggs.

"Oh, leave that there." Emma slipped inside with a handful of fresh cut flowers. "Sarah Douglas told me if I left it across the pan, the water wouldn't boil over."

"Really? I'll have to remember that, if it works." Angel noticed a small sunflower in the midst of Emma's bouquet. Instantly, she pictured Brennan's house. She'd never been inside, yet her imagination painted a clear picture.

"Colton told me you had off this morning. You could spend the day with me. Mrs. Davis needs to finish fitting my gown."

Emma's soon-to-be mother-in-law had insisted on making Emma's dress. Angel was happy for her and the relationship she already had with her future family. Would she get along with Brennan's mother as easily?

"Angel? Angela?" Emma waved a hand in front of Angel's face.

"Oh, sorry. What did you say?"

"You must have some heavy thoughts this morning. I asked if you wanted to accompany me in the wagon."

Angel appreciated the invitation, but knew how much Emma enjoyed Mrs. Davis's motherly attention. "I don't want to intrude. How about you drop me off at Juliann's? She and I haven't had many opportunities to visit lately."

A couple hours later, Angel waved as Emma continued down the road then turned toward

Juliann's front porch. The door flung open and Sammy hopped down the stairs. "I told Mama we had company. Hi, Miss Reese."

"Hello, Sammy. You've taken a growth spurt. Soon you'll be as tall as your daddy."

"Nope." Sammy straightened to his full height. "I'm gonna be taller."

Angel's laugh was joined by Juliann's. Her friend motioned for her to come in. "What's in the basket?"

"You can't tell by the smell?" Angel waved the towel and the smell of boiled eggs permeated the room. "Emma said we were getting too many, so I've brought lunch."

Juliann waved a hand in front of her nose then ran for the door.

With the basket left on the table, Angel followed. "Are you okay?"

"Yes, the smell just made me nauseous is all."

"I understand. They do carry an awful odor."

They stepped off the porch and meandered through Juliann's thriving garden. Angel bent to smell a patch of lemon grass, appreciating its freshness.

"I heard about yesterday's rattlesnake … and Brennan's rescue." Juliann smiled knowingly. "Isn't that the second time he's saved you?"

A smile stretched across Angel's face. How much should she tell?

"Are you still having your dreams?" Juliann's question didn't leave Angel time to decide.

"Since Brennan saved me from the coach and snake, I haven't dreamed about those incidences."

"Good."

"Maybe."

Juliann stopped at the start of her herb garden. "Why do you say that?"

"If they have to happen before the dreams go away then there's still going to be a stampede."

Juliann was the only one she'd confided all the dreams to. Her friend grew quiet as she picked several leaves of peppermint. "Tell me again about the other dream, the newest one."

Angel closed her eyes to capture the images. "I'm in an unfamiliar building. I don't know where it is, but it smells old and dusty."

She could almost feel the rough, hard surface she leaned against and hear the sound of heavy footsteps. "I'm with people that are somewhat familiar, but I can't place them."

With a glance at Juliann, she said, "I recognized one of the voices and thought I'd remember when I woke this morning, but I didn't."

"Was it Brennan's?"

"No." She tried to control the instant smile that tickled her lips. His was a voice she wouldn't forget.

"Why are you rubbing your wrist?"

Angel looked down and realized her action. In an instant, she was back in her dream. "My hands are tied. There's a lot of commotion … then I always wake up."

Juliann now stood near her, her eyes full of concern. "Are you scared?"

"Yes and no. I'm aware of facing death, but at the same time I'm filled with peace."

Red blotches formed on Juliann's face as her eyes swam with tears. "How can you speak so calmly about it? Doesn't he save you?"

"I'm not sure." Angel clasped her hand over Juliann's. "Like I said, I always wake up from the commotion."

A sob hiccupped past Juliann's lips. "You make it sound as if you might die."

Chapter Ten

Angel crinkled her brow as she studied Juliann. She wasn't usually emotional. Something more was upsetting her friend.

Before Juliann's spoken concern, Angel hadn't dwelled on the possibility she could die. The dream did unsettle her, and she hadn't been rescued, but … her chest tightened … would God call her home so soon?

For Juliann's sake, Angel had to be confident. She pulled her into an embrace. "Julie, don't cry. Whatever happens, I'll be in Jesus' care." She said the words without thinking of the true reality.

She'd been taught Heaven was better than anything she could imagine. But when life was good and full of expectation, it was hard to fathom leaving it behind.

"I know. I know that in my head. It's just hard to accept in my heart." Juliann pulled back and wiped her eyes with the back of her hand. A long sigh shuttered from her chest. "Added to this upset is another … Robert and I are expecting."

Air rushed from Angel's lungs. "Julie, that's wonderful!" Her friend's damp eyes were etched with worry "Why are you still crying?"

"This isn't the time to bring a baby into the world." She swatted at a bee as it buzzed by. "I don't even know if Robert will be here when it's born."

Angel wasn't aware of any problems between Juliann and Robert. Juliann wasn't making any sense. "What do you mean?"

"The Lincoln telegrapher barely escaped with his life. If it weren't for that last message, why he would've …" she cried harder. "What if that happens to Robert? What if there isn't a reason for him to leave the office and he's inside when they blow it up?"

Tears stung Angel's eyes. How could she respond? Although, like Clara, Juliann's fluctuating mood was probably due to her condition, her pain was evident. Angel wanted to give her worries the attention they deserved.

Juliann wiped her eyes on her apron. "I've not been myself lately. I've been sick each morning and get emotional over the smallest things."

Angel looped her arm through Juliann's and heaved an exaggerated sigh. "Between you and Clara, you make pregnancy sound lovely." She joined Juliann's immediate laughter.

"You needn't worry, Julie. Brennan won't let anything happen to Robert."

Juliann's somber mood returned. "He can't be everywhere."

Angel considered her latest dream. But regardless of the vague outcome, Brennan would save her. Why else would her dreams lead her to consider her rescuer as her *future* husband?

Juliann spoke again. "Not that I've joined in any of the conversations, but there's talk in town. The folks are growing restless because of the increase in thefts." She lowered her voice as Sammy rounded the corner of the house. "If Brennan can't stop those …"

"I need something to drink." Sammy, his hairline damp with sweat, stood beside their faithful dog, Shep.

"Yes, let's go inside and cool off." Angel saw the peppermint still in Juliann's hand. "And I'll make you some tea. That should calm your stomach."

Angel heated water for the tea then helped Sammy quench his thirst before he rushed outside to resume his adventures with Shep. "Remember what the pastor said Sunday about trusting God? I can speak from experience that it's not always my first response. Our feelings have a lot of pull, and it's natural to hold onto things and want to fix them ourselves."

The struggle she still battled toward Savannah made what she was saying all the more needful. "But if we truly trust God to work His will in our lives, then we need to leave our burdens with Him."

"I know that's what I should do." Juliann cocked her head to the side as her eyes changed focus. "What's that on your wrist?"

Angel's chest lightened. Finally, she would get to share with someone. "My reason for needing the same encouragement I shared with you," she smiled, before explaining.

***

Brennan finished feeding the prisoners and returned to the office. Neither Colton nor Harris had arrived. He stood in the doorway and scrutinized the town as it woke from a quiet slumber.

More than once, he caught himself staring toward the corner across from the diner. Angel was late. Usually if something held her brother up, she walked to work. Worry nagged at Brennan's gut. It didn't use to be this way. Although for some time he'd counted on seeing Angel in the diner, he hadn't worried over her. Somewhere over the last year that had changed. Would he ever relax about her well-being again? Probably not. At least not until she didn't have to work. But because of her desire to buy her own home, she was determined to stay employed.

He recalled Angel sharing her dream while he took her home. His home was the goal each paycheck fueled. Funny how all the times he caught her admiring it from across the street, he never considered the reason why.

A thought teased Brennan's heart. If they married, she'd get the house and not have to work, which would ease his worries. But was that reason enough to propose?

He rubbed a hand over his face. Walking Tall saw what he'd been blind to for too long. Brennan had feelings for Angel. Feelings that grew stronger each day.

Movement across the street interrupted his reflections. His uncle, Michael Hall and his son, Robert, emerged from behind the bank and approached the jail. Their clothes were wrinkled from keeping guard throughout the night, but otherwise, they appeared unaffected.

Uncle Mike shook Brennan's hand. "I'm glad you're having men from the town take these shifts. We're certain someone was up to no good last night."

Robert took over. "We heard a horse snort back in the woods behind the bank. It wasn't long before a shadow emerged."

"We don't know if he saw us or what his intentions were," Uncle Mike stifled a yawn, "but he didn't approach us or the bank."

Brennan ground his teeth. "It's going to happen. Whoever's behind this isn't letting up."

Robert cleared his throat. Brennan turned as Harris strolled toward them.

Harris eyed the two watchmen. "You boys must've slept in a barrel."

A desire to rearrange the man's toothy grin had Brennan's fingers fisted at his sides. "Nice to see you decided to show up this morning, Deputy."

Harris glanced from side to side. "Seems to me I made it in before Colton. Guess he needed more beauty sleep."

Brennan ignored the man and turned to his family. "Thank you, Uncle Mike, Robert." Dismissed, they left for their homes.

"Can't your watchdogs solve your problems for you, Sheriff?" Like a prickly porcupine, Harris knew how to provoke others, but Brennan refused to react, at least not until he understood how Harris became aware of privileged information.

"What do you mean by watchdogs?" Had the Lincoln man been the shadowy figure spotted last night?

Harris's grin faltered.

"Sorry for my late morning." Colton rode up beside them and hopped to the ground. He led his gelding toward the stable in back. "My herd got out this morning. Wasn't aware of it until halfway to town."

"Did you figure out how?" Harris licked his rolled cigarette and sealed it with his thumb.

Colton scoffed as he shoved past.

"Harris," Brennan threw out the first item on the list to keep Harris at bay while he had a chance to talk to his deputy, "check in with Mr. Sanders, make sure everything's square at the bank."

If Harris suspected Brennan was onto him, the job he tossed out should confuse the culprit just enough to slip. At least Brennan hoped. He took a risk trusting the man to enter the bank, one he hoped he wouldn't regret.

Then again, he had no proof Harris was up to anything illegal.

Brennan found Colton waiting for him at his desk.

"Is the snake gone?"

"Yeah, I sent him to the bank."

The size of Colton's eyes matched the ring of his coffee mug sitting on the desk.

Brennan would have laughed if not for the seriousness of the situation. He waved him off and skipped an explanation. "What's got you so worked up?"

Colton reached into his shirt pocket. "Whoever cut my fence was careless enough to drop this." He withdrew a stubby roll of tobacco, the same brand Harris rolled only moments earlier.

***

The noon sun burned overhead as Brennan ignored his hunger pains and paced his mustang beside Harris and Will Jackson's horses. As the farmer of several hundred acres, Will rarely came to town, which made his sudden appearance at the jail moments earlier reason for alarm.

Will spoke around a toothpick held between his teeth. "I should've come in earlier, but the boys got stirred up against you and to tell the truth, after chasing my cattle back from three separate stampedes, I was sharing their opinions."

An aggravated sigh tore from Brennan's chest. Until this morning, none of those he'd spoken with about the loose cattle had suspected foul play. Mr. Jackson should've come to him sooner.

"Only after coming in today did I realize I'd been at fault."

"At fault?" Brennan centered his attention on the weather-beaten farmer.

"I was in sore need of more men out there with the cattle. In a fix, I hired a feller about a head taller than you, Sheriff ... despite a bad feelin' about him."

An image of the blonde man at the river came to mind.

"He didn't last long. After the mess with the cattle he tore off. I came in for business today and while I was at the diner, I heard about the robberies. Then it connected."

Brennan spied Harris from the corner of his eye. The reason he'd brought the deputy along was to stay aware of his whereabouts while duties drew Brennan away from the bank. The mouthy deputy rode quietly with an unnerving contentment.

Brennan rubbed his trigger finger against the inside of his palm.

At the start of corralling loose cattle, the town began complaining of petty larceny. From Will's information, it was safe to surmise the tall figure was to blame for his cattle stampeding. Could one of the other men Brennan spied at the river be blamed for the thievery? The facts were adding up, but where did Harris fit in?

As the third man?

"The herd!" Will cried. "And there's the varmint I told you about, Sheriff."

Brennan followed the direction Will pointed. A tall form rose high above the worked-up cattle. As if aware he'd been caught, the cowpoke scrunched toward his saddle.

They had to apprehend the suspect before he worked the cattle into a full panic. Brennan touched his heels to Condor's sides. The eager paint dug his hooves into the ground then sailed across the grassy plain as though never touching the ground. With his thighs tightened around the equine's middle, Brennan stayed afloat in the saddle, his movements matched with the horse.

Realizing his fate, the culprit turned directions. His horse reared, dropping the cowhand's hat, then ran toward a wooded lot. Brennan withdrew his pistol as his mustang narrowed the distance. The ground passed by at an incredible speed. The cattle became a blur to the side. In moments, Brennan would have the blonde giant apprehended.

Condor snorted and tossed his head, throwing off the perfect balance of horse and rider. Brennan tightened the reins and settled deeper in the saddle.

Without expectation, the paint changed directions and tore through the slowing herd. Brennan yanked the bit in the horse's mouth. No response. He ground his teeth. Cattle bumped against his knees as their eyes rolled with fear. If he didn't get control of his mount, they could very well start a stampede of their own doing.

Brennan glanced over his shoulder. Harris continued in his place. Doubts nagged his gut before Condor came to a sudden halt.

The loss of momentum lurched Brennan forward. He grabbed the saddle horn with one hand while the other shoved back against the mustang's neck. He landed back in his seat as the horse tossed his head and stared overhead. Brennan followed his skyward glance and saw a bird of prey circling above.

Was this some type of Indian omen? Walking Tall's words came back to him, *"Great Spirit says you will need Condor. He will guide you on next journey."*

He tightened his jaw. *Maybe his journey to the afterlife!*

Condor snorted and took off to the south, following the bird's flight.

Brennan growled beneath his breath and fought to control the crazy animal. As a last resort, he considered jumping onto the back of a nearby steer. He might get more accomplished than with the brainless horse he'd unwittingly traded for.

What felt like hours later, but in reality was closer to minutes, Brennan reined Condor beside Harris and Will.

"What was that all about?" Anger and frustration laced the farmer's words.

Brennan slid to the ground, his legs and stomach sore from fighting the bull-headed paint. He left the horse breathing hard from his run and walked away. If he didn't, he might give in to his anger and put a bullet between his eyes.

He inwardly kicked himself. Not every trade was a win, but never had he lost this bad. He stared at the sky now free of vultures. Condor. The name made sense. Walking Tall was wise to keep the information to himself. Had Brennan known, he'd never agreed to the trade.

"I need a new horse."

Harris rode up beside him all teeth and smiles and dropped Condor's reins next to Brennan. "Say, you got a fast little paint there. Too bad he has no sense of direction."

Brennan glared at Harris then at the expended horse, the cause of his humiliation and failure. With reluctance, he grabbed the reins and saddle horn and noted the missing outlaw. He spoke to Harris as he swung a leg over the saddle. "No surprise you let him get away."

"Don't worry." An evil glint shined in the deputy's eyes. "The one responsible for this mess will pay. I'll make sure of that."

The one responsible ... Brennan was certain they weren't talking about the same person.

Chapter Eleven

Brennan washed his face and hands in his kitchen sink then fixed a plate of dinner. Although he longed to see Angel, thanks to Condor, his dirt-coated appearance kept him away. The best thing to do this evening was stay home and wash away his foul mood. His stomach soured at the thought of his horse. How was he supposed to protect the town with an animal he couldn't control?

He bowed his head for prayer then lifted his fork and knife to cut into the pork steak. As he sawed through the overcooked meat he blocked the irritating animal from his mind. But as soon as he was free, Harris's image appeared and ruined Brennan's appetite. Sick to his stomach, he left the table. Although he hadn't eaten since breakfast, he wasn't hungry.

Harris had to be dealt with … and soon. But what charge could Brennan hold against him? He was certain the sly fox was leaving a trail. And one way or another—Brennan ground his teeth—he'd find it.

Harris hadn't come back with the cowhand. This only fueled Brennan's theory. If Harris was the third gunman, naturally he wouldn't apprehend his own man.

The stampedes and thefts made for a clever distraction, built in their favor. Eventually, one of the distractions would pull Brennan from town, leaving the bank free for the taking.

He stomped through his house to the porch. Angel stood across the street in her usual diner attire of white shirt and black skirt. His heart lifted at the sight. The screen door squeaked on its hinges as he pushed it opened and made his way toward her.

Her mint green eyes sparkled as he drew near. When had he noticed their color?

"Good evening, Sheriff."

His mouth pulled in a slow smile. He could listen to her sweet lilted voice all day if given the chance. "Why aren't you at the diner?"

"They didn't need me." Her gaze dropped to the boardwalk.

"The Meyers didn't need their best waitress?" What were the Meyers thinking?

"With Savannah's presence, they thought I could use a morning off and come in for dinner. Only when I came in tonight, they said I could take the rest of the day off, too." She swallowed and eyed her open reticule. With a snap, she closed it and stared again at his house.

Her dream was slipping from her fingers. He also considered his home. For the first time, he saw his dwelling from a different perspective. The two-story white clapboard was a handsome design. Well-furnished and comfortable, what had he been thinking when he put it up for sale?

Brennan held out his arm. "Mind joining me on the porch?"

Two dimples formed beside her mouth as her eyes moved from him to the rockers. "Those were my favorite chairs at the store."

As they crossed the street together, Brennan smiled and winked. "I know."

After retrieving his glass of tea and filling one for Angel, Brennan rocked beside her and breathed a sigh of contentment. He'd imagined this very setting numerous times since purchasing the chairs.

Angel rested with closed eyes, but a constant smile played on her mouth.

"What are you thinking?" Brennan itched to know.

She kept her eyes closed as her smile grew. "Just imagining I was home."

His heart stilled. Of course she would be. This was what she wanted. He steeled himself and ventured to ask, "And where would I be living?"

"Well, here—" Her eyes popped open as crimson climbed her neck and cheeks.

Brennan didn't think his smile could stretch any farther. He touched her hand. The charm clinked against her glass. "I think this would be better worn around your neck." He unwound the chain.

Her eyes fluttered before she turned for him to clasp it behind her. "What will I say if someone asks who it's from?"

"Tell them the truth." He met her sparkling eyes as she swiveled back in the chair. "Walking Tall gave it to you."

Angel's eyes lit with humor before growing serious. "I can say it's from you, can't I?"

He nodded then leaned closer. "You sure you like this house? It's not very private."

***

The next morning, Brennan stifled a yawn between mouthfuls of biscuits and gravy. At least this was something he couldn't mess up. As the eldest child, his mother had taught him early on how to care for his siblings should the need ever rise.

He hadn't been to visit for several weeks now. Not since receiving news about the robberies. His mouth watered for Mama's Sunday roast. As soon as he wrapped up this case, he'd take a day to visit.

A smile tugged at his heart. He'd ask Angel to join him. Her visit yesterday stirred a growing desire to spend more time with the blond haired angel. She knew his parents, and he was certain they'd be proud of his choice.

After checking in with last night's volunteer watchman, Brennan found Colton already in the office.

"How long do you want to hold Kurt and Ben?" Colton rested the empty breakfast tray against the wall. "You know it's always the same routine."

Brennan massaged the building tension in the back of his neck. It was thanks to those two roughnecks that he had a past with Sarah Douglas. In an effort to leave an unpleasant situation, she'd innocently answered an ad for a wife, only to learn she hadn't been writing Brennan Douglas, but two clowns bent on getting even with the sheriff. Slow learners. Their foolish antics often earned them jail time and a fee.

Colton paced to the door then back to his desk. "They've learned nothing from our usual punishment."

"I agree."

"It's time to try something different."

It wasn't often Colton took the lead. And from the spark in his deputy's eyes, Brennan was sure he had an idea, one he was anxious to hear.

"They need positive relationships with leading men from the town." Colton paced the room as he spoke. "Instead of a fine, make them earn their freedom through acts of repentance with those whose property they've vandalized. Who knows, it might seep through to their hearts."

"Do you still meet on Saturday mornings to pray with Uncle Mike and others from church?"

"Yes."

Brennan nodded in consideration. "Then we'll make them attend as well." There was more than one way to clean up a town.

"Sheriff," The telegraph message boy's eyes darted around the room. "Mr. Hall would like to speak to you … about a telegram."

Brennan met Colton's steady gaze. He was sure his deputy held the same anticipation. News from Lincoln?

Once there, Brennan accepted the wire from Robert. He read over the note sent from Sheriff Douglas then struck a match and lit the corner of the paper. He stomped the charred remains on the floor. He couldn't risk giving Harris a lead.

"Wire back," Brennan lowered his voice in case anyone was close enough to overhear. "We'll meet tonight. After dark."

Robert nodded and tapped out the message. Within moments, Sheriff Douglas replied in agreement.

The Lincoln lawman had something to share. Something worth waiting at his telegrapher's side until his message was confirmed and important enough to meet in person. Brennan thanked Robert, then paid and left the office. Time wouldn't tick fast enough to day until Sheriff Douglas shared his knowledge.

His gut instinct told him to be on edge, evil lurked close by.

Angel. Brennan had to warn her. Her innocent nature could land her in the middle of something dangerous.

After the breakfast meal, Brennan found her clearing tables.

"Hi, Sheriff." She still called him by title. Maybe it was time to change that.

"Oh, Sheriff," Savannah entered through the kitchen. "I missed you stopping in yesterday. I suppose you was out saving the world."

Brennan clenched his jaw. Her presence never helped him win confidence with Angel. "Not exactly, Ma'am." Although it was an understatement, he wasn't about to explain his fiasco with Condor.

"Angel, would you mind stepping outside with me a moment?"

Angel nodded, her face tight with concern.

He shot a look of appreciation toward Savannah. "You'd cover for her, wouldn't you?" He knew she wouldn't say no then led Angel through the kitchen and out the back door.

Brennan watched her worry her lip. He lifted the chain around her neck, sliding the charm between his thumb and finger. "Relax. Nothing's changed."

A visible sigh lifted from her shoulders. "Are you here on business?"

He nodded and gave a description of the men he saw at the river. "Have they stopped in here?"

"Once, last week." Her throat constricted. She hadn't felt comfortable with them.

Brennan's chest tightened. He took her hand, unconcerned for the spying eyes of Mrs. Meyer. "They're dangerous men, Angel."

"They just ate and left."

He rubbed his calloused thumb over her smooth skin. He'd saved her twice. But with the trouble brewing as it was, he worried not being there if she might need him again. "Tell me about your dreams."

She broke eye contact. Her hand fluttered to the charm. "I have." Her actions confirmed his fear.

"What *aren't* you telling me?" His heart thumped harder.

"Have you ever had God speak to you through a dream?"

Blurred images of Walking Tall and Condor came to mind. He'd expected to meet the Indian on the road, all from a dream. "Yes … sorta."

"Then you know they're not always clear."

"But some of your dreams have come true." He ran a hand across his jaw. "If there's more you know is going to happen, you should tell me."

She stared into his eyes. Brennan fought to keep focused and not drop his gaze to her lips. Angel cleared her throat. "I've had two others. The first one is a stampede."

His stomach hardened with her omission. If not for her other two dreams already becoming reality, he'd hope this one simply stirred from the recent cattle activity. But he knew better. "What happens?"

Angel shrugged a delicate shoulder. "You reach out and save me."

Her smile didn't build his confidence. Too many *what ifs* worried his thoughts. "What of the last one?"

The air, thick with humidity, draped over them like a blanket. Angel wiped her forehead, her demeanor changing to fear. She turned and hid fidgety hands inside the pockets of her apron. "That one still isn't very clear."

Brennan moved closer and rested a steady hand on her shoulder. "Help me out, Angel. I want to be there for that one, too." He felt a slight shudder run through her frame.

"I don't know where I'm at in the last one … but my hands are tied …"

Brennan's world darkened with dread as he listened. *God, don't let this happen. Give us a chance to build on what You've given us.*

When she finished, he turned her back around to face him. He smoothed a hand down her cheek. "I'll be there. God won't let us down."

"Brennan."

There was his name again. He wished she'd always use it.

"Whether you are or not, I'll be okay." She gave a slight upward glance.

He shook his head and refused to accept the innuendo. *No, God, you can't take her.* Despite who might be watching, Brennan pulled her to him. He kissed the top of her head as she sighed against his chest. *But if this can't be changed, guide me to where she'll be.*

***

The air stirred around Brennan as he rode across the uneven terrain to meet with Sheriff Douglas. He'd left town several hours earlier to throw off anyone who might try to follow. Although he'd only heard of three men involved in the robberies, riffraff had a way of attracting the same. There were others who, for the sake of a quick dollar, would be willing to take on menial tasks. And Brennan had plenty of enemies who would line up for the job.

He'd allowed Condor to stretch his legs across the river plain, but now slowed him to a steady trot. A three-quarter moon gave enough light to see by as they kept a steady pace with two miles left to go.

A snake rattled and Condor shied to the side. He snorted and pawed the ground.

"Get moving or get bit!" Brennan urged the horse forward.

Condor refused to respond. He snorted again and half jumped, half pawed, closer to the snake. Brennan easily visualized the snake coiling tighter as its rattle became more pronounced The horse was asking to get bit, and Brennan didn't want to walk.

"Move!" He kicked his heels in the equine's sides. A half whinny squealed from the horse's throat as he leaped forward and took off in a panicked run. Brennan didn't know if the animal thought he'd been bit or if the tense situation added to his fear. But nearly a mile later, Brennan convinced him to slow down to a walk.

He leaned forward to rub Condor's neck and pulled back. His hand was matted with hair and sweat. This horse was a peculiar animal. Brennan was sure he'd wanted to pound the snake with his hooves. But in the dark, his chances of success were drastically smaller than if it were daylight.

Not long after, he saw the flame of a match in the spot he and Lincoln's sheriff used for their meeting grounds. It hadn't been too long before that they'd met here every week while planning the take down of the murderous Frank Ferris.

Brennan rode up as Sheriff Douglas extinguished the flame between his lips. Douglas wasn't a man to wrestle with.

The sheriff leaned his forearm across the saddle horn and cleared his gravelly voice. "Glad you could make it."

"I take it your telegrapher is all right?"

"Yeah. Still upset over his office, but we're building a new one. Thanks for the loan of the machine. You'll be mighty glad you sent it once you hear what I've got to say."

Chapter Twelve

Curious as to why the lawman couldn't have ridden to Warsaw with or without a telegraph machine, Brennan waited for Sheriff Douglas to continue.

"I found out a few things. Makes me sorry I ever sent you Harris."

Brennan had suspected as much when he'd received Douglas's wire. He ground his teeth. *Give me a reason to toss the suspicious snake behind bars.*

"When Edwards was hit, Harris and I and much of the townsmen had been fighting a wild fire for a couple of days. We still don't know how it started, as it was before this heat wave." He ground out the next words, "I suspect foul play.

"Anyway, the more I think about it, I can't account for Harris's whereabouts during most of the fire. In fact, one of the bank tellers mentioned a smell of wood smoke in the vault after the robbery."

Brennan didn't move as he listened to Sheriff Douglas. Was Harris behind each of the heists? He'd be glad if the answer was yes, but only if they could prove the theory without doubt. Despite how little he respected Harris, he'd never want to arrest an innocent man.

He shook his head. "Not that I want to defend Harris, but we have to view this case from every angle. It could be the fellows who started the fire were the thieves, not necessarily Harris."

"Hmmm ... only Harris didn't show until a couple hours after we'd returned to town."

Close by, a pack of coyotes yipped and howled. Douglas's steed pawed the ground and stepped backward. "Hush up, you ole' coward." The older sheriff, though he sounded gruff, bent over and rubbed the horse's neck, encouraging him in a quiet tone.

For once, Brennan felt a certain amount of pride in his painted mustang. The horse had yet to show fear toward anything. He stood motionless ... possibly asleep.

Sheriff Douglas continued, "Then we have the lone robber in Gravois Mills. Harris was reportedly away for his sister's funeral."

"I didn't think he had family."

"He doesn't. At least not anymore." The moonlight glinted off Douglas's hard jawline. His stoic stature made him a threatening figure and reminded Brennan of when they rode together in the posse. Even though Brennan had been the one to form the group of men, Sheriff Douglas had been an excellent guide, teaching the younger lawman more than years of experience had proved.

"Remember Frank Ferris?" The name was spoken with disgust and deservingly so.

"How can I forget?" Brennan forced himself not to dwell on the past and its disturbing images. Ferris had been the mortal form of the devil, carrying out deeds too heinous for your average criminal. "What does that murderer have to do with the robberies? The court sentenced him to swing. And we were there when it happened."

"True." Douglas straightened his shoulders. "But they didn't sentence his brother, Henry Ferris, better known to you and me as ... Deputy Harris."

The weight of his words squeezed Brennan's soul with an apprehensive grip. The crimes Frank committed weren't that of a sane man. If Harris was half as evil as his brother ... "How do you know?" Brennan hoped he was wrong.

"Had one of my men check the records in Kansas City. They were complete with pictures. There's no denying it, we've been hooked and all this time he's been reeling us in. The question is, for what?"

Brennan shook his head as thoughts bombarded his mind. "It can't be just to rob the bank. Could it?"

"I'd say he's been saving the best for last. Everyone knows you're the hero who brought down the most notorious murderer in these parts. How much does Harris know about you ... about your family ... about your town?"

Brennan leaned forward in the saddle as his stomach rolled. *Angel.* Did Harris know how much she meant to him? Aside from her, who else would the criminal mastermind target to even the score with the man responsible for his brother's death?

Images of family members flashed before his eyes.

Brennan didn't wait for the Lincoln sheriff to say more. He reined his horse around and kicked his heels into his sides. Condor sparked to life and sailed across the uneven terrain as if he'd been waiting for the moment.

What Douglas said meant Harris had a plan.

The satchel and the paper Savannah had found. They needed to find it and quick.

***

Once home, Brennan pulled up a chair at the front window. His nerves on edge, he didn't bother trying to sleep but took watch. Although he had two men positioned behind the bank, he didn't want to take a chance on missing Harris should he choose to show himself.

Brennan's mind swirled with possible scenarios and his heart pounded with fear while his head argued from a logical angle.

For all his disdain toward Harris, the man had yet to show a truly evil side like that of Frank Ferris. Brennan gripped the rifle rested across the arms of the chair. *Don't let him be like Frank.* If there was a chance, Angel would be the target. He swallowed hard against the certain acknowledgement.

At first light, he'd check in with Colton and the banker then investigate the area around the cave again. Although he doubted the culprits had been back, if there was a track, it might lead him closer to their new hideout.

He rubbed a hand over his tired face. The Osage River had numerous bends. They could be hidden anywhere.

His eyelids drooped as his thoughts drifted from the cave, to his family's farm, to a stampede. Cries for help called out to Brennan, but they came from every direction. He'd never reach them all in time. But who did he help first?

His chest tightened. His breaths shortened. He was going to fail. He couldn't save them all.

A rooster cried at the edge of town startling Brennan out of his chair. He rushed to his feet with the rifle raised and pointed. Holding the gun steady, he listened again.

"Cock-a-doodle-doo!"

A dizzying coldness swept over him as he fought to make sense of his surroundings. At some point during the night he'd fallen asleep, but not for very long. A fog permeated his brain and weighed against his chest.

A cushioned fainting chair his mother insisted he buy tempted him to fall into its cradled form and sleep. Brennan took a deep breath of resistance and scanned past the windows, catching the edge of the diner.

In an instant, his body was charged with the energy of a thousand head of cattle. Clarity flushed his senses, returning them to full alert. Rivulets of excitement pulsed through his veins. No time to rest. He had to protect Angel and his town.

The streets had stirred to life when Brennan approached the jail. He met Colton at the door. "Has Harris been in?"

"No." Colton rose from his chair as Brennan hung his hat. "The longer you took getting here, the more I thought the worst."

Brennan's mouth pulled to the side. "You think that puffed-up turkey can best me?"

Colton's expression lacked all signs of humor. "I think he's sinister enough to try."

His deputy's insightfulness snaked a path of dread down Brennan's back. He motioned for him to step outside where he informed Colton of his meeting with Sheriff Douglas.

Colton's face lost its color as his shoulders sagged against the wall of the building. He rubbed one hand across his pants leg while shaking his head. He'd stepped in as deputy after the last one had been shot and killed ... by Ferris.

Brennan slapped Colton's arm to draw him from thoughts that would only cloud their focus. "Come on. Let's make the most of our time."

They followed the local boardinghouse owner, Joe Conner, into the bank and waited to speak to Mr. Sanders.

"T.J.," Brennan shifted his weight to one hip and spoke in hushed tones, "it's time to prepare for the worst."

"Already done." T.J. stomped the floor boards beneath him. "Didn't trust that fellow, Harris."

Brennan pictured the safe the town council voted be installed below the floor after the Edwards and Gravois Mills robberies, accessible only by a secret panel. "How much?"

"Nearly all. Left out enough to take care of day to day transactions—" His voiced faded as another patron stepped through the door.

Colton nudged his chin and made small talk with Mrs. Jackson, allowing Brennan to continue with the banker.

"Harris is definitely not to be trusted." Brennan shook the banker's hand. "You have good instincts. Continue to follow them. They just might save your hide and this bank."

He turned to leave then stopped. Brennan couldn't stand the thought of the banker's family losing him. Still controlling the volume of his voice so not to alarm Mrs. Jackson, he added, "If you're held up, offer the keys and get everyone out. Let them do what they want once you're gone. Just get out."

Brennan hoped T.J. had taken him seriously enough to do as told, because he couldn't give him the real reason for the order. If anyone suspected a connection between the robberies and Ferris, the town would seize with fear.

After checking the back of the building, Brennan and Colton rode through the wooded acreage behind town, and emerged at the river where he'd previously spotted the three men. The worn path disappeared in the sandy gravel.

End of the road. He squinted against the sun, straining to find where they might have hidden a skiff.

"It's safe to assume they're hiding across there somewhere." Colton rode past as he spoke, peering at the other side, "We need a boat to get across and keep searching."

"Can't do it." Brennan ground his teeth. "If we turn our backs that long, we'll come back to empty accounts."

"Do you think Harris ever showed up today?"

"No. He probably had someone watching me and knew I took off last night. He's crafty ... which makes him all the more dangerous."

Brennan longed to investigate the area, but time wasn't on his side and he couldn't risk being away a full day. Not anymore. Not until they had Harris behind bars. "Uncle Mike and Robert made good deputies in times past. I think I'll have them scout downriver toward the inlet. See if I missed anything."

"Or I could bring Savannah out here. Maybe she could point out something we missed. Something she might have seen the day she found the satchel."

Despite Colton's serious expression and good intention, the sheriff wasn't fooled. Anyone could see Colton was attracted to the newcomer, but her safety came first. "Find a different reason for spending time with Savannah. Don't take her anywhere outside of town. If Harris's men are watching, she'll become their next target ... if she's not already."

The idea ate at his thoughts as they returned to town. Savannah had found the pouch. If they suspected she'd read the paper why hadn't they made an attempt against her?

Brennan urged Condor to pick up speed. Perhaps the paper meant nothing and he was wasting time concentrating on the wrong clue. He sighed heavily. *God help me.*

Once in town, the late lunch hour was announced by the line of patrons exiting the diner. Perfect timing. Brennan never liked eating in a full house. Not only were there too many people to keep a safe eye on, Angel couldn't spend as much time at his table.

He pushed open the door to the diner as Angel finished taking a customer's order. Their gazes locked and scenes involving their future teased Brennan's imagination. A satisfied sigh floated from his chest as she smiled before turning back to the kitchen.

He and Colton took their regular seats. The smells of fried chicken and baked cobbler triggered his saliva glands. Brennan inhaled. Yesterday's skipped meals had left their mark. He could devour anything set in front of him.

"Hope it's calm tonight. Emma's fixing dinner, and out of the three girls, she always was the best cook." Colton scanned the diner until settling on the long haired waitress.

A frown pinched Brennan's forehead deep enough he could feel the puckered skin. No longer concentrating on food, he rubbed his thumb across the nicked edge of the table and ventured to ask, "Is Angel going?"

"Of course." Colton continued to stare across the room. "With Savannah here Sis can afford to take time off."

But does she get a choice? Since Colton was obviously enamored with the temporary waitress, Brennan withheld his thought, not wanting to cause problems between siblings. His mind on other things, Colton probably never considered asking his sister how she felt.

Angel arrived at their table, unable to control her smile or the radiating glow about her. "Two specials?" The light reflected off the pendant around her neck as she glanced from her brother to Brennan, where her gaze remained.

Colton turned to nod in agreement to her question and jerked his head to the side. "Was that Mama's necklace?"

She ducked her head and returned her glance to Brennan. "No."

Before Colton could ask, Brennan stated, "I gave it to her."

Colton dropped his jaw. "When—"

Cecil stopped by the table and touched Angel's arm. "See you tonight, Angela."

Tonight? *Angela?* Brennan's hands curled into fists.

Chapter Thirteen

Brennan returned Cecil's challenging smirk with a hardened stare. Whatever the farmer had going for him wasn't enough. If Angel had wanted him, he'd have already won her hand. Brennan rose from his seat and followed Cecil out the door.

The man stepped off the boardwalk and pivoted around. "Just because you wear that badge doesn't mean you can stop me from seeing her."

Standing several inches taller than Cecil, Brennan relaxed his stance to ease his opponent's concern. Warsaw had enough trouble to deal with. He didn't need Cecil's anger complicating matters more.

"I don't need to stop you. She's smart enough to choose for herself." He held out his hand in an offer to shake. "May the best man win?"

Narrowed eyes drilled into Brennan. Cecil glanced behind the sheriff to the diner and back. His jaw relaxed before sighing, "Fine." He shook hands. "Her happiness matters most."

Brennan watched him retreat before returning inside. Poor Cecil knew nothing of Angel's feelings. The man could never make her happy. A woman like Angel thrived from being around others. All Cecil would do is stuff her in a lonely house far from everyone she knew where she'd wither like a flower in a cold snap.

Once at the table Colton fired off the questions from earlier. "Angel? *My* sister? When were you going to tell me? I wouldn't have agreed with Emma to invite Cecil had I known?" Colton's mouth pulled into somewhat of a grin.

"Yeah, right," Brennan answered in mock belief before settling his long frame into the polished chair. "You thought you'd heat up the situation with some competition."

"You're right." Colton's expression grew serious. "And you're also *right* for her."

Angel returned with their orders. She glimpsed at Brennan before her eyes did an apprehensive dance toward her brother. "Will that be all?"

Brennan's tongue seemed to swell in his mouth. He hadn't mentioned courting to Angel, but that's what her brother had insinuated. Knowing she could very well respond like Juliann, the thought of Cecil asking her first gave him the courage to take the risk. He inhaled deeply, took her hand and urged her to sit in the vacant seat. "Not in the least." He nodded toward his deputy. "It seems I have to ask your brother an important question."

A giggle escaped Angel. Did she know what he was about to do?

"With your permission, Deputy, I'd like to court your sister."

Colton smiled and peered from Brennan to Angel. "Is this what you want?"

Light seemed to radiate from her eyes as she nodded her head. "Definitely."

Her brother's brows drew together as he pinned her with a stare. "And not just because of your dreams?"

Brennan held his breath as Angel's upturned mouth straightened into a line. "Colton, I have more common sense than you credit me. Trust me," she turned to face Brennan, "this is the only man I'd agree to court."

She lowered her voice. "And it's not because of his house either."

He returned her smile and pictured her leaning against the post across the street staring at his house. The image quickly changed to Angel in the kitchen. Brennan saw himself walking up behind her, wrapping his arms around her middle and trailing kisses from her temple to her lips.

"I didn't know they'd arranged for Cecil to come to Emma's."

Angel's soft confession replaced his dreaming with harsh realism. Cecil had won her company for tonight.

She stood, needing to return to work. Brennan pulled her to a stop. "Just don't enjoy his company too much."

Her eyes shimmered from what he hoped was an inner joy. "You know I won't."

***

Angel forked another bite of her sister's roast dinner. The rosemary rub had been a secret of their mother's, but despite Angel's best efforts, she couldn't remember the exact recipe. Each time she asked Clara, her sister always pretended not to recall one or two of the ingredients. Angel suspected it was her way of assuring her siblings willingness to gather together. None of them could turn down an invitation for the meal, not when it brought with it such fond childhood memories.

"Remember the time you told Pa you'd already fed Jasper but you hadn't?" Emma pointed her fork toward Colton. "Then when we sat down to eat the ornery mule shoved his head through the back door and brayed right in the middle of Pa's prayer!"

A ripple of laughter surrounded the table. But as much fun as the evening had been, Angel couldn't help but imagine Brennan seated beside her in replace of Cecil.

She worried the hem of her shirt sleeve. Cecil's smile was never as relaxed as her favorite lawman's.

Brennan was a man who took his job seriously, even watching the patrons of the diner with duteous concern, but could also let loose a roll of laughter that made those around him enjoy the humor more fully. Cecil's tight smile quickly resumed its normal state of a frown. Angel didn't understand his interest in her. Their personalities couldn't be more different from one another.

She retrieved her water glass and brushed against Cecil's hand. "Excuse me," she whispered. Despite her best efforts to pretend not to notice him, his penetrating stare burned through her. Didn't he understand she wasn't interested in him more than a friend?

Todd cleared his throat. "I'm sorry we can't stay longer. I promised Father I'd help him with the store's paperwork this evening."

They all rose and saw Emma and Todd to the door. As the couple's wagon faded down the road, Colton announced, "I settled on their wedding gift."

Clara frowned. "You're making the decision without us?"

"A Malable Range. We all know they'll need a stove. And Miss Luella will sale us her used range for less than half of a new one."

Miss Luella, one of their beloved Sunday school teachers from youth, always thought of special ways to show love and concern, even more so after their parents' deaths. Would Clara agree? The idea was nice, but would require more than Angel had hoped to pay.

Colton continued, "The gift would be from Miss Luella too. Which leaves only five dollars apiece from each of us."

"Well," Clara waited for her husband, William's, opinion.

"Your decision," he answered.

Angel fingered the charm around her neck. If things with the sheriff progressed as she hoped, there wouldn't be any need to save for a house. A wave of relief lifted from her shoulders. The idea of buying a home on her own had been more challenging than she'd originally realized.

"I'm in. I think it's a lovely idea." Angel smiled at the thought of Emma opening the gift then pulled her mouth to the side.

"What is it?" Colton frowned.

"How will we wrap it?"

Everyone laughed … but Cecil. What would it take to lighten his serious mood?

"Angel," Clara cleared her throat. "Perhaps Cecil could bring you out again on Saturday?"

Angel lifted her gaze to Colton. Surely he would help her out. He knew of Brennan's intentions. Poor Clara wasn't aware as they'd had little time to discuss anything without the presence of Cecil. The man hadn't left her side for more than two minutes the entire evening.

"I believe she has to work, Emma." Colton came to her aide.

Relief washed over her. With a polite smile, she gave Cecil a quick glance.

"May I walk with you outside, Angel?" Cecil's request held an intensity that made her squirm.

She strained toward the dining room. "I should help Clara with the dishes. Perhaps later?"

"The dishes can wait, Angela." Clara's stern motherly voice took control.

Angel closed her eyes for a brief moment before accepting Cecil's hand as he led her out the door.

Where would he begin? Angel couldn't lead him on any further. He was a nice man and a sure catch to someone … just not her.

"Would you mind sharing your thoughts?"

What would Brennan think if he saw our joined hands? That probably wasn't what Cecil wanted to hear. Angel cleared her throat in time with a bull frog near her sister's pond. She laughed and saw that Cecil had actually smiled. "That wasn't me," Angel explained, thankful for the lighter moment.

"Wouldn't matter if it was. I'd still be here with you."

Angel swallowed and groped for a safe place to start conversation. Clara and William's farm lay two miles from town. And somewhere close was Cecil's. "Does your land connect with William's?" As an excuse to pull her hand from his, she pointed down the road.

"On the back side." He moved her pointed finger toward the back of his brother's property as he continued leading her through the yard. "It's on the farthest side from town. I think it's the perfect distance. Makes me think ahead when purchasing supplies and allows me more time to do the things I'm supposed to do. Town can be too distracting. Don't you agree?"

Angel peered straight ahead. "Actually, we differ in that area quite a bit. I look forward to a day when I can live in town."

Cecil's steps slowed. "You do?" He scratched his chest right below his throat. "I never imagined—guess I figured you'd be glad to leave the restaurant."

Angel shrugged. "I like being around people. I like listening to what they have to say and seeing them in town, especially in the mornings when everyone's greeting one another. Don't you enjoy the company of others?"

"I enjoy your company." He stepped closer. "I'd enjoy keeping you all to myself someday, too."

A small gasp slipped by her. He sure didn't waste any time. Angel moved back a step. "That's nice flattery, Cecil. But you work long hours. What's a girl to do all by herself during that time?"

"Housework, I su'pose. Don't you sew and garden and like to clean?"

Angel almost giggled. Is that all he thought a woman dreamed of doing? "I think we should head back to the house before—"

A horse and rider galloped toward them. Cecil grasped her hand. "Come on. It could be important."

They returned to the house as Clara's husband was getting ready to leave. "Something spooked a large head of cattle out toward the Holt farm. They need all the extra hands they can get."

Cecil promptly followed the other men.

Colton paused long enough to say, "Take the wagon, Angel. I'll meet you at home."

Angel joined her sister at the door as the men hurried off. A shiver raced down her spine as her dream came back to haunt her. Spooked cattle could only mean a stampede. She turned toward the kitchen. "Let's hurry and clean this up. Then I'll head home."

The man hadn't mentioned what direction the cattle were, but she was certain danger was headed their way.

Clara dried the dishes until she dropped into a nearby chair. "Sorry I can't keep up."

"Don't be. You made a delicious meal." Angel worked on the last pan.

"You were quiet tonight." Clara fiddled with a stray strand on the hem of her apron. "Are you upset I invited Cecil?"

"Not at all. I half expected you would."

"Then why so quiet?"

Angel hesitated to say anything. The conversation would prevent her from leaving as soon as she'd like. Not that she didn't want to visit one on one with Clara, but she also didn't want to get stuck in a nightmare.

"And where'd you get that necklace? Is it from Cecil?"

Now she had to explain or risk Clara asking Cecil. "It's from Brennan. He's asked to court me."

Clara slapped the table, just like their dad used to do when he was surprised. "When did this happen?"

"Earlier today."

"Why am I always the last to know?" Clara leaned back and rubbed her abdomen. "Do you really think he'd make a good husband? Cecil is a steady man, dependable too."

"And lacking in personality." Angel bit her tongue a little too late. "I'm sorry for saying that, but—"

"I know, it's true." Clara pointed a finger. "Sheriff Brennan on the other hand, probably has too much."

Angel smiled and shook her head. That was one of the things she found so charming about Brennan. His confidence was an admirable trait. Not afraid to stand up for what was right, despite the opinion of others.

Like with the recent murmurings in town. Some thought the sheriff was falling behind on his duties, but Angel knew better. He and Colton had been anything but slack. Working often until after dark, they strove to keep Warsaw a safe town.

"Are you still having dreams?"

Angel cringed. *Here we go.* "Yes, and Brennan fits in them perfectly."

Clara withheld comment and took the towel from Angel's hands. "That's enough cleaning for tonight. You'd better head home while it's still daylight."

Although it wasn't like Clara not to state her opinion, Angel wasn't about to argue. "You're right."

Clara leaned against the flour hutch and sighed. It wouldn't be long before she'd make Angel and Emma aunts. The idea sent a flutter of excitement to Angel's heart. She hoped her turn at motherhood wouldn't be long in coming.

Moments later she headed home over the rough dirt road. Although the humidity had steadily built throughout the week, it had yet to rain. Plumes of dust billowed up behind the mule's hooves and into Angel's face. She pulled on the reins. "Slow down, Jasper, before you fill my lungs with dirt."

The mule grunted in complaint.

"You'll still get your oats, don't worry."

Angel watched the trees pass by with dreamy eyes. Each one stood as a suitor from the past. None of them had been acceptable. Too tall. Too stout. Too loud. Too brash. She'd refused them all, even before her dreams had begun.

Jasper turned at the fork in the road that led to town. There in the very corner of the divide stood an age-old hickory. Its broad branches spread wide to offer shade to weary travelers and its sturdy trunk withstood the nailed signs directing which way led where.

In many ways, Brennan was like that tree. As sheriff, he helped keep Warsaw a safe place to live. And unlike sheriffs of the past, he was never satisfied to just arrest those who did wrong, but often made them attend church in hopes of leading them down a better path.

Jasper swung his head and strained to see behind them.

Angel followed suit. Nothing but an empty road. "It's only us, Jasper." The mule picked up pace. This time Angel didn't stop him.

She glanced over her shoulder again but saw nothing.

They reached town as the sun began to wane and Angel sighed with relief. Just a mile on the other side and they'd be home. A dog began to bark followed by another, then another. Jasper brayed and pulled harder. "What's wrong with you, boy? Dogs don't scare you."

Angel frowned and watched the wagon seat. A new sensation traveled up her legs to her arms. Something like a ... vibration?

A cow bawled and a thundering sound shattered the air. Angel's heart fell to her knees. She didn't need to turn around to know what was there. Jasper's legs moved in a blur. Led by fear, the mule raced for home.

The thundering hooves sounded closer as the noise of the stampede ricocheted off store walls. They'd destroy the town. The streets emptied as folks ran into shops, dropping whatever was held in their hands. Horses tore loose of posts and sprinted down the road.

Angel screamed as the frightened cattle penned her in on either side.

Dust filled the air. Wood splintered and popped. Angel dropped the reins and grabbed the wagon seat to keep from falling. Heat from the stampede closed around her in waves.

Beside her, the round eyes of a steer rolled with fear. He bawled as another pushed past him. More wood popped. The wagon creaked and moaned …then dropped to one side.

Chapter Fourteen

"They're heading to town!" Brennan roared over the deafening sound of cattle then coughed to clear the dust-filled air from his lungs. Whether or not the other men heard, he was certain they were aware of the dreaded reality.

Condor responded to every command, but it hadn't been enough to tame the panicked four-hundred head herd. Brennan recognized Will Jackson from a neighboring farm as he rode ahead and banked his horse against the frenzied cattle, snapping a whip over their backs.

Much to Brennan's horror, instead of the cattle changing direction, the man and horse were absorbed into the herd. If Jackson didn't work his way out he'd be trampled.

Brennan leaned over his horse's neck, "Fly, Condor."

Just when he didn't think the horse had anything else to give, the mustang let loose as though fresh from the gate. As if sensing the danger of the other horse and rider, Condor quickly closed the distance separating them.

Will's face held a grim expression, one that said he'd accepted his fate, only Brennan wasn't about to let him.

"Get ready to bolt!" Brennan yelled over the pounding hooves and withdrew his sidearm. With the gun held over his head, he fired off three shots. The sudden explosion frightened the cattle closest to him causing them to veer to the side. Will saw his opening and steered his horse to safety.

Without time to stop, Brennan continued to steer the stampede. If they could maneuver them in a circle they'd tire out and eventually stop. He fired off his remaining shells and saw others doing the same. While he fought to reload, an unmoving figure appeared in his side view. On the rise of a nearby hill, Walking Tall stood repeating the same motion with his hands.

Brennan growled beneath his breath, "I don't need this. Either mount up and help or let me work." With some reluctance, Brennan gave in to an inner urge to take his eyes off the herd. Walking Tall repeated the same motion with his hands. He acted as though he was picking something up then turning and giving it to an unseen person to his side. Once done, he repeated the motion from the beginning.

I don't have the patience for this. We have a herd to ... Angel! The Indian repeated the motion of giving her the necklace. Brennan's heart stalled in his chest. What could Walking Tall mean? The herd had changed direction. Angel was no longer in danger.

A shout rang out from one of the men. Brennan looked back. A hundred head broke free from the herd and continued toward town.

How could the Indian have known?

Condor responded with a quick turn and followed after the fading herd of cattle. Running with renewed speed, it wasn't enough to get ahead.

A lump lodged in Brennan's throat. "Get me there in time, Lord."

Angel's dreams had been given to her for a reason. Because of His grace, God had granted Brennan a door into the future. He knew what had to be done only his horse wouldn't hold out at this speed for long.

A memory from years back jumped to the surface. Past the creek was a forgotten trail, a shortcut of sorts to town. Few knew of the overgrown path. Would he be able to find it?

Moments later, Condor crashed through dry brambles and jumped across fallen logs. The equine seemed to sense the same urgency that surged through Brennan.

A deer skittered to the side. Brennan caught a glimpse of its white tail before dodging a low branch.

They finally tore through a side street as the sound of the herd's destruction grew. With only a couple of yards to go, Angel's wagon raced past with cattle penning her on either side.

Brennan leaned forward. It had worked once before, he hoped the mustang had enough stamina left in him to respond in kind again. "Fly, Condor."

With a short shrill, Condor rounded the corner and onto the boardwalk. From their elevated position, Brennan saw Angel clinging for her life on the bench seat.

Something cracked. Then popped. Fear gripped Brennan as the wagon lolled to the side.

"Now!" he commanded his horse as he reined him toward the stampede.

Condor jumped into the mass of bodies, stumbled, and righted himself to escape being trampled. Brennan reached toward Angel as a cow ran beneath his arm.

"Angel! Jump!"

Her face ashen, Angel tore her gaze from the cows to him. As if in a moment of shock she didn't move, only stared as though he were an apparition.

A pop sounded as the other wheel snapped off and dropped the back of the wagon on the ground. Hooves pounded the dragging wood.

"Angel, honey, you have to jump!"

In an instant, Angel gathered her skirt and leapt into Brennan's outstretched arm. He kept her momentum and swung her into the saddle sideways.

The mule brayed as the cattle clobbered the ramp made by the wagon. He'd be drug beneath their hooves in a matter of seconds.

Brennan aimed his pistol around Angel's side. His first shot missed the hitch but heightened the panic around them. Angel clung to his neck. He aimed again as a steer climbed into the wagon bringing the mule's front feet off the ground. The shot connected and splintered the hitch.

Condor raced ahead through the throng of hooves, pushing his way out the side. Angel's breath whispered against Brennan's neck, "We made it! And Jasper, too."

***

Once the cattle were corralled, the dust settled revealing an ugly aftermath. Brennan leaned against the wall of the boarding house with Angel still trembling by his side. Pieces of boardwalk littered the road. Shingled porch tops hung over the front of store faces like curtains pulled for the night. One by one, curious souls emerged from the backs of buildings to survey the damage.

A dog wiggled loose from his boy's arms and whined as he sniffed the ground then barked in Brennan's direction. Condor's nostrils flared wide with each exhausted breath he inhaled, but otherwise didn't move.

The town wasn't ruined, but would take the collaboration of its occupants to rebuild what had been destroyed.

Brennan pulled Angel closer and kissed the top of her head. "Someone's going to have to keep you awake so you can't dream anymore."

She relaxed against him. "But you were here. Just like God told me you'd be."

He swallowed hard. "Am I in the last one?"

Before she could answer, a distant yell broke the town's shocked silence. Brennan rolled his head against the side of the building and listened. It came again, only closer.

Angel pushed against him and stepped toward the street. "Did he say—"

Sara Douglas rushed toward them and grabbed Angel's hand. "The bank's been robbed!"

Renewed adrenaline fired through Brennan's veins. Before he was aware of his actions, he started running forward and met the boy responsible for the news.

"What do you mean?" How and why waited on the tip of his tongue.

"They blew off the back." The boy panted from excitement. "They must've done it when the stampede came running through."

From the safety of stores and businesses, men joined him in the street, running to see what they didn't want to believe.

Brennan slowed as the bank came into view. The truth was visible through the busted windows. The sky and forest from behind showed straight through the building.

T.J. limped toward him. Brennan caught him by the arm and saw the open wound on his leg. "Get this man to the doctor!"

"Sheriff," he winced with pain. "I saw him. Harris. It was him and two others …"

"Was anyone else hurt?" Brennan helped balance the banker as he answered.

"No. I did what you told me. I just couldn't move fast enough." The color faded from his face. "I heard them out back. They were going to blow it with us inside."

Two gentlemen looped T.J.'s arms over their shoulders and helped him to Dr. Jenson's office. Brennan whistled for Condor, determined to track the thieves through the woods.

Part way down the path, Brennan turned back at the sound of pounding hooves. "Daniel. Robert." He slowed to a stop as his cousins caught up.

"You can't do this alone and expect to succeed." Daniel's brows drew together in disapproval.

Brennan agreed but assumed most of the men were still fighting the stampede. Thank God for these two. "This path leads to the river. I doubt we'll catch them before they hop a skiff, but maybe we can trail them down stream."

They hurried beneath the canopy of leaves until it opened wide to river and field. Condor tossed his head. The scent of water teased his senses. Brennan eased from the saddle and let the animal move ahead to take a well-deserved drink.

Upstream, the smooth surface of the water flowed with a weight of disappointment. They couldn't be that far behind the culprits, where was their boat? Brennan, joined by the other two men, walked the bank for signs of three horsemen.

Robert shook his head. "Are you sure they came this way?"

"I'd hang my hat on it." Brennan followed signs of hooves ending at the bank, remounted and urged Condor into the water. "We'll swim across and check the other side."

Robert urged his mount to follow. His horse tossed his head and refused to cooperate. Brennan smiled at the comical scene before tensing as cold water filled his boots and climbed his legs. He quickly withdrew his rifle and sidearm and held them above his head, doubting the wisdom of his decision.

Condor blew from his nose as water circled around their necks. Brennan kept hold of the horse's mane as they made their way across the calm water.

On the other side, Condor shook his entire body then tossed his chin back to smack Brennan's leg.

"I didn't like it either." He holstered his guns then removed a boot as water poured out of the leather sewn pitcher. The ground withheld any clues. Not a print to be found and downstream the river widened. With a tired horse, there was no way he'd want to chance making it back across.

Was it possible they swam in the direction of the cave? He hollered across to the opposite bank where Daniel and Robert waited. "I'll follow the inlet and meet you back in town."

Daniel shook his head. "No you won't. We'll follow the inlet on this side and meet up at the end."

He'd never convince them differently. And although the cave was protected by a tall bluff on their side, if fire did open up, he'd appreciate knowing they were close enough to help.

Blanketed by woods, Brennan led Condor a few yards back and trailed beside the water. After what seemed like fifteen minutes, he pulled to a halt and listened.

Above the water on an overhanging limb, a red-winged blackbird sang from his perch. Other birds tweeted notes as they flew by.

Brennan listened for Daniel and Robert. When he couldn't hear horse or man he retrieved his binoculars and focused across the water.

Climbing the ridge, both men on horseback came into view. He scanned the perimeter for any unwanted visitors. Satisfied with their safety, Brennan returned the lenses to his saddlebag and nudged Condor forward.

They hadn't trekked very far when he noticed the muddy bank marred with … hoof prints. Condor tossed his head, either aggravated at the constant stops or sensing the presence of others.

Brennan eased his pistol from his side and readied the hammer. The trail led into the forest. How far, he didn't know. The cave was still another half mile to the end of the inlet.

A trickle of sweat left a zigzag path down his temple.

Time was against him. With less than an hour of daylight, to take the path now would lead him into their hands. Brennan gave one more glance toward the wooded trail before moving on. God willing, he'd return at first light.

Chapter Fifteen

Brennan and Colton returned to the path the next morning with well-rested horses. No clues were found in the cave, but like his father always told him, anything worth having was worth working for. This case was proving that wisdom true.

Angel was also worth working for. He'd almost lost her more times than he'd rather remember. Even as he laid his head to rest last night, recollection of her fear-filled eyes continually woke him.

He sought to replace the memory of her fear. "How's your sister this morning?" Colton would know who he meant.

"I told Emma to let her sleep in. Can't imagine the diner being busy after yesterday. At least not this morning."

"Good call." In his opinion, Angel's ordeal should earn her the week off.

They came to the path and Brennan dismounted. Squatting low, the prints proved no one had returned. He peered at Colton. "You ready for this?"

Colton squared his shoulders. "Let's get it over with."

***

Angel brushed her hand across the broad tops of Queen Ann's Lace as she walked to town. The hearty wild flower grew in abundance along the dirt road. Already late, there was no sense in hurrying.

Something tickled her palm. Angel turned her hand over and screamed as a spider scurried to the other side then up her arm. "Get off! Get off!"

She brushed it to the ground then stomped her feet and shuddered. That would teach her to leave the flowers alone.

"Lord Jesus, I don't think I can take any more." Her pounding heart drummed against her chest. She drew a deep breath. Not even her prolonged sleep had eased the adrenaline still pumping through after yesterday's stampede.

She needed Brennan. His strong arms and confident voice would drive her fears away. Angel wished they were married. Then she could stay in his beautiful house, safe and secure, and not have to go to the diner.

Deep in thought she walked on until the outskirts of town emerged before her. Angel hadn't realized how much ground she'd covered. A thought nagged in the back of her mind. Why did she care about going to the diner? After all the time she spent there, it was like her second home.

Still the nagging feeling wouldn't leave.

People milled about with purpose, hauling away the ruined store fronts and hammering nails into the new. A strange feeling hung in the air. Angel took a closer look at the folks she passed. No one smiled and greeted, "Good morning." Not even the children laughed or frolicked.

It was as if the stampede had also trampled their spirits.

"We need a sheriff who can do his job."

"He did put an end to that murderer a few years ago."

"Can't run an office on one win. What's he doing for us now? We're ruined. The town will shrivel up and won't be fit for anyone."

Angel covered her ears to keep from hearing more. How could anyone speak ill of Sheriff Brennan? He'd devoted his life to keeping this town safe. She couldn't bear to consider the numerous times he and Colton had put their lives at risk for Warsaw's residents. All of this because of the stampede?

She hurried past, too emotional to speak. Tears fought escape as she stopped outside the back door of the diner. After taking three deep breaths, she found the courage to step inside and serve a public that had lost faith in her hero.

"I don't know what we'll do." Mr. Meyer, her employer who rarely voiced his opinion on anything, beat batter in a bowl at the worktable. "That money helped keep the town alive. Why most of us kept our life savings there."

"Not you, too?" Angel's disheartened voice drew the attention of both her employers and Savannah.

Mrs. Meyer hurried over and wrapped her in a soft, warm embrace. "Sweet girl, I'm so glad to see you. We hadn't heard if you'd been hurt or not."

Her concern broke through Angel's weak defenses. She sobbed on her employer's shoulder.

"It's okay, honey. You've been through so much."

Angel sighed as the last hiccup left and pulled back. "I'm sorry."

"No need to be. You weren't hurt none?"

"No. Brennan saved me ... and my mule." She gave a feeble smile then straightened her shoulders. "I've heard a lot of talk against Brennan."

She eyed Mr. Meyer. "You weren't saying things, too, were you?"

Mr. Meyer moved beside her and placed his chubby, flour-covered hand on her shoulder. "What do you mean people are talking against him?"

She sniffled and dried her eyes on the underside of the apron Savannah offered. "The people working on the town. They're so disgruntled."

"Well, we'll see about that. Don't you worry none, your sheriff will set things right."

Angel blinked and stared wide-eyed at Mr. Meyer.

"Of course we know." He winked and went back to his batter, followed by his smiling wife.

"It's as empty as a cave in here." Savannah took Angel's arm and guided her toward the diner. "Don't worry about being late. Ain't no one been here."

She bent to pick up a linen napkin that had dropped to the floor. "I figure it's 'cause folks are already counting their pennies with the bank robbed and all."

The bank! That explained the town's loss of hope. Angel sank to the floor against the wall.

"Angel, you okay?" Savannah bent near her.

"Brennan won't be able to set things right without the money. The town's turned against him and he'll risk his life to get their money back."

Savannah dropped her gaze to the hardwood floor. "Colton too, I suspect."

Angel met Savannah's eyes as she brought her head up. The pain she saw was a mirror reflection of what her heart felt. Would they both lose their chance at love?

She patted the floor at her side.

Savannah slid to the floor. Sadness pulled at the corners of her mouth. "I thought I fancied that sheriff you're so fond of. But he never made my heart dance a fiddle quite like yo'r brother."

Angel smiled as all previous jealousies flew from her heart. "God's in control. All we can do is stay vigilant in prayer."

"You know my Whinny is well now. I can go home anytime."

Their conversation had changed everything. Angel found herself caring whether Savannah was happy or not. She no longer wished she'd leave. "Do you miss home?"

"Not as much as I should." She stood up and wiped down an already clean table. "It's fun livin' on my own … well, not exactly on my own. But with the Meyers. They treat me like a daughter only I don't have a bunch of siblings to keep up with."

"I guess your mom will want you home."

"Yeah, she already wrote asking when I'm coming. I'm second oldest. And with Nellie already gone and married, and the next couple kids being boys, she needs my help." She sighed heavily. "I should head home in the next couple of days."

Angel soaked in the information with some regret. Having been caught up in jealousy, she'd never considered to ask Savannah about her family. How would Colton receive Savannah's departure?

***

Brennan slapped his palm against the trunk of a tree. Another trail that led back to the beginning. He slid from his mount and tried to walk off his aggravation.

Harris and his men had planned the stampede as a cover while they robbed the bank. But that was only the beginning of their crafty scheme. From there, they hid their trail with the river and then ran circles in the woods to throw off any pursuers.

As sheriff, Brennan had only dealt with one other man as crafty as this. Frank Ferris.

Colton emerged from a separate path. His scowl attested to the same failure rate. Their entire day had been spent running circles. "Next option?"

Brennan tongued his cheek then grimaced. "Face the town." Considering all that had transpired, without a lead he'd been seen as a failure.

The arrival was met with one of the council men. He rose from a chair seemingly positioned to watch for coming visitors ... or just Warsaw's returning lawman.

"Hanover." Brennan nodded and pulled Condor to a halt. Colton stopped beside him.

"Sheriff, the town's called a meeting. And you're the guest of honor."

What more did they expect him to do? Brennan fought the anger rising inside him. "Lead the way, Councilman."

Daniel met him outside the courthouse. "I tried talking to T.J." He kept his voice low to keep from being overheard. "In light of the other bank robberies, I'm certain you would've told him to use that floor safe you installed. But he won't spill a word about it. I hope for your sake it wasn't all in the vault, or the council will chew you up."

Great. It was all on him. T.J. could've saved him a lot of trouble and told them, but if Harris learned he hadn't gotten it all, he might come back. *God, lead me.*

Once inside the small room, Brennan became the center of attention. Two hours passed before he finally satisfied the men's growing disdain. Yes, they still had their money, which T.J. attested to. No, he hadn't caught anyone responsible for the robbery or the stampede.

"One thing's for sure," Brennan moved toward the door. "The day isn't getting any longer. If you want the men responsible, then leave me to do my work!"

He stormed from the room.

* * *

Brennan shuffled into his house, weary from a day of worthless scouting. He'd gone back and searched with Colton, and now both of them were too baffled to think straight. They needed time to recollect and pray.

He removed his gun belt and laid the bullet-filled rawhide on the empty side board. He stared at the desolate furniture then turned to take in the rest of the room. The house could use a woman's touch. He'd built it with Juliann in mind, thinking she would enjoy filling it with doilies and quilts and whatever else women did that turned a house into a home.

But that hadn't happened. The house was still just a house.

Angel would change that. The idea had merit and brought a smile to his dirt-laden face. He hadn't been able to spend nearly as much time with her as he wanted. But God willing, once he arrested Harris and his men, all of that would change.

He gazed toward Heaven. *There's another good reason for You to help me out here.*

After a cool bath and donning clean clothes, Brennan felt human again. Only he still hadn't received any heavenly direction.

"Sheriff Brennan!"

Brennan hurried to the front door at the sound of a woman's panicked voice. What had happened now?

"Hurry," Savannah tugged on his arm. "Colton's been knocked out and Angel's gone."

Angel's gone? Fire surged through Brennan as he took off at a run, nearly dragging Savannah with him. They arrived at the diner where the Meyers were attending to Colton. Mrs. Meyer began crying as she dipped a towel in a bowl of water and dabbed at the swelling on his deputy's head. "They took her. She barely got a scream out," she sniffed and choked on her words, "and then they were gone."

Out of habit, Brennan went to palm the butt of his handgun, only to realize he'd left it at the house. He forced himself to slow down. The next move he made could be the most vital for Angel.

"Did you see anyone?"

The owners of the diner shook their heads, while Colton was still out cold.

"Mr. Meyer, get Doc Jenson." Brennan turned to Savannah. "Did you hear anything at all?"

Her bottom lip quivered. A tear trickled from her eye before she sputtered, "It was supposed to be me."

"You?" No. She was wrong. Harris nabbed Angel to get to him. "Savannah, I need to know if you heard them say anything."

She nodded as bigger tears rolled down her freckled cheeks. "I heard someone say they were here for the ... the w-wench that took their bag." She covered her face in her hands. Sobs shook her shoulders. "I heard just as Angel had stepped out."

Mr. Meyer slipped past to get the doctor and nodded for Brennan to follow. Once alone, he said, "I didn't know she'd heard anything. She'd slipped back in awful fast though."

Brennan ran the facts through his mind as he watched the cook disappear around the corner. Fear had caused Savannah to hide rather than help. Not an admirable reaction, but understandable given her youth and reason to be afraid. But if they were here for Savannah, then she must have something of theirs.

He rejoined her in the kitchen. Savannah stood unmoving, her attention centered on Colton.

Brennan checked his pulse. "He's been through worse. He'll be fine."

Savannah blinked and took a deep, shuddering breath. "I know why they want me."

Brennan narrowed his eyes. Why did he have a suspicion she'd been keeping something from him all along?

"I feel terrible." Her eyes pleading, she begged, "Please believe me. I didn't know I had it."

Irritation had Brennan grinding his teeth. Angel's life was in danger. If Savannah had something worthy to say, now was the time.

"It must have fallen out of the satchel into my bag. I didn't know until I was packing to go home."

"What? What fell out, Savannah?"

"A ... key."

Chapter Sixteen

Brennan stared at Savannah as his world spun to a halt. If the key she claimed to have belonged to Harris, the devil of a man wouldn't stop until he had it back. Prickles of dread climbed Brennan's spine. "Where is it?"

Savannah slipped a hand into her apron pocket. "I was going to give it to you when you came in today. Only, you never did." She opened her palm, revealing the aged, forged iron.

Brennan turned the key over in his hand, noting its simplicity. Despair settled like a heavy weight on his chest. If they needed this, they'd do anything to get it back.

He swallowed before speaking, yet despondency still laced the edge of his words. "Several years ago, about the time we captured ..." Brennan stopped before naming Frank Ferris. If anyone in town realized the connection between him and Harris, panic would overturn Warsaw, complicating Angel's rescue.

Brennan cleared his throat and continued, "A kid said he found an old safe in the woods. He described it as having three key holes in the front."

"One ... for each ... thief." Colton tried to rise before dropping his head back.

Savannah dropped to her knees beside him as his eyes closed again. She shook her head and sniffed. "Where's the safe now?"

"We never found it." Brennan stared at nothing as the clock in the diner ticked a reminder of the passing time. Aside from an act of God, he didn't stand a chance of finding the safe. And since he figured it was the safe containing gold bars Frank robbed from a train several years ago, Harris and his men were no doubt holed up in the same place.

He glanced at his silent deputy. These villains weren't the kind of men you battled alone. Although he didn't want to endanger his kinsfolk, considering the circumstances, they'd expect to ride beside him.

Colton struggled to rise again. Savannah placed a hand on his chest. "Stay put. You're not in any shape to ride."

He moaned and succumbed to her demand.

Doc Jenson entered, followed by Mr. Meyer, and sat his medical bag on the floor beside Colton. Brennan waited long enough to hear him mention something about good vitals then slid out the door before his struggling emotions were revealed.

Fear for Angel gripped his heart with a suffocating pain. Was she hurt? Scared? The description of her dream was pure torment. If Harris laid one hand on her ... Brennan pictured his gun as his tightened grip dug the key into his hand. Angel's safety relied on him keeping calm and holding onto rational thoughts. He couldn't give into fear—or rage.

Moments later, after securing his gun and holster to his side, Brennan raced from the jail toward his uncle's.

Without waiting, Brennan threw open the door. "Uncle Mike!"

His cousin, Ruthie, screamed and threw a hand to her chest. "Brennan, what's going on?"

Aunt Kate raced into the room. "Michael isn't home from Robert's. They were checking fence—"

"They took Angel." Brennan rushed back outside as his voice cracked with the mention of Angel's name. Cutting through the field, he quickened his time toward Robert and Julianne's farm and hoped to catch both men at the house.

***

"Stop moving, wench!"

Angel stilled as a large hand slapped the back of her leg with a menacing strength, stinging her skin. Her body trembled from her head to the soles of her feet. Thrown across the front of a horse like a sack of grain, Angel's head continually bounced off the side of the abductor's boot. Motion sickness gripped her insides. Added to the jarring movements was the putrid smell of the bag tied around her head. Angel fought to keep her stomach from recoiling by concentrating on the rope around her wrists.

The knot had been tied in haste, providing enough simplicity to work the rope loose. The hardest part was keeping the slack while continually tossed. Angel wriggled her wrists back and forth until it felt her skin would light on fire. The horse leapt over a log and crashed back to the ground.

Angel's stomach surged, and she made one final pull.

Free! She pulled the offending bag off her head then coughed and gulped for fresh air. She sputtered and held her nose. Nothing was fresh this close to the man's feet.

Ahead, rode another horseman. Where were they taking her? Tall grass whipped her face and jabbed at her eyes. Angel turned her head and strained to see the owner of the smelly boots.

With her head craned as far as she dared without drawing another slap from the evil man, she peered upward. Her vision seemed to climb forever before stopping on the blonde stoke of hair glinting in the moonlight. *Goliath!*

Shivers raced across her skin as her last dream became engulfed in reality. They were taking her to their hideout … where they would again tie her hands.

It didn't take long for the next stage of their journey to begin. The horse slowed and a man shouted from somewhere close by. That voice? Angel had heard it before. Just like in her dream, the sound was familiar but she couldn't place the owner.

Her abductor's large hands scooped her up like a rag doll and tossed her from the horse. Angel landed with a thud before her head hit the ground. An ache pounded the back of her skull as stars twinkled in her blurred vision. She blinked and a familiar face stooped over hers.

"You brought the wrong girl!"

Angel scrambled back. Small stones scraped her palms and fingertips. Harris's white teeth shone like a snarling wolf in the sparse moonlight. With a sharp movement, he grabbed her ankle and yanked her toward him.

Angel wouldn't go without a fight. She raked as many stones and dirt she could into her hand. As her adversary reached forward she flung it into his face.

"Ahh!" Harris turned his head to protect his eyes.

Angel flipped around and raced toward the cover of trees, but Harris was too quick. His hands closed around her like a steel trap.

He tossed his head back and released an obnoxious laugh. "This will work just fine." Despite her constant struggling, he dragged her toward a decrepit building. Light from a lantern glowed between missing boards. As they approached, Angel saw most of the far side had already fallen in.

Harris tossed her in a corner. Mold spores shot from her cushioned landing adding to her already nauseous stomach and her leg throbbed from the whelp left from Goliath, but she wouldn't give any of them the pleasure of knowing.

Like a wild animal, Harris's eyes drilled into hers as he tied her hands together again. "Unlike my brother, I've never taken pleasure in killing a woman ..."

Angel's breath stalled as his words sunk in with mounting fear. He didn't say he'd never killed a woman, just ...

"But if your sheriff doesn't deliver," he finished tying her hands with an unnerving gentleness, "I'll make sure he'll never forget the way you died."

Angel didn't move. Nor did she blink. The evil glaring from Harris's eyes held her in place. It was as though the devil himself was trying to take a bite of her soul.

Angel snapped her eyes shut. She belonged to Jesus. Satan couldn't have her. Like a child's timid voice, she whispered the beginning verse to Jesus Loves Me. As she found confidence in the Spirit, her voice strengthened giving power to each melodic word.

Harris spat and stepped back. Within moments, the men had all left the barn.

Angel finished the song then continued to sing others she'd learned in the booster choir at church. Thank God for sweet Miss Dorothy and Miss Luella. Their dedication to the children had forever sealed melodies of comfort in her heart.

***

Grant us grace, God. Brennan remounted after scouring in vain for a track of any kind. Once more, he'd lost the trail at the river.

"What if we're too far?" Robert pulled up beside Brennan. "I'm going to backtrack and see if there's a trail leading off from the diner."

Brennan could barely bring himself to nod. They were losing too much time. Angel had told him that in her dream she wasn't afraid. Brennan knew it was because she was at peace with whatever God ordained. *But I'm not. Don't take her, Lord. I'm not ready to let her go.*

Uncle Mike reined beside Brennan. "What's your instinct telling you?"

Pain burned behind his eyes. Rarely did he allow anyone to see his weakness, but Uncle Mike knew too well what was at risk. Brennan forced himself to stare directly at the man. "I don't know. I've explored every area that makes sense."

"The safe was supposed to be across and to the east of the river, right?"

Brennan nodded.

"Then forget about finding a trail. Head that direction. I'll follow and Robert can wire Sheriff Douglas." Uncle Mike nudged his horse and spoke as he rode away to tell his son.

Brennan strained against his weighty chest and took a deep breath. More to himself than his uncle, he asked, "But what if I still can't find it?"

"Then follow your h—."

Brennan frowned as he too rode away. Had Uncle Mike said heart ... or horse?

***

A mile later, Brennan still hadn't found the safe. He swallowed past his dry throat. Angel had been gone for over two hours. He swiped his brow. Instead of a reprieve, the humidity only increased with the lengthened day. They were in for a downpour. Brennan strained to find a trail before a sudden cloudburst hid it for good.

Condor snorted and pranced to the side.

Brennan yanked the reins. Condor shoved his tongue against the bit and fought for the lead. A shadow flew over them and Brennan's hopes plummeted. Vultures should've already nested for the night. Why was this one still soaring?

Condor reared before taking off in a charge. Brennan locked his knees against the crazed animal and fought a useless battle for control. The animal forged a path through the rocky terrain, weaving around the occasional tree and vaulting over small gullies.

When at last he slowed, Brennan jumped to the ground, anger tightening every fiber of his being. His foot slipped on the uneven terrain and sent him to his knees. With a grunt, Brennan caught himself with his hand as his thumb slid into a curved indentation. He glimpsed at the dirt and traced the groove with a relieved sigh.

A hoof print.

Condor snorted and tossed his head in the direction behind Brennan. Brennan swiveled around. A path led toward a wooded thicket. He stared at the grove. Each time he'd searched, he'd somehow skipped this area. The lay of the land kept it tucked away from common passersby.

Dusk settled heavily as Brennan entered the forest, masking any hopes of visibility. "All right you smart-aleck horse, you got us this far, lead the rest of the way."

Condor flicked his tail, whipping Brennan's leg. Brennan ignored the obstinate gesture and peered through the trees for any sign of life.

Something flickered ahead. Brennan withdrew his rifle and dismounted with only the creak of his leather saddle. He looped the reins on a branch and climbed over a crumbled rock wall.

A lone chimney stood in the middle of shrubs and briars, giving him enough cover to survey the rest of the abandoned farm.

Dark clouds blew across the moon leaving scant light. Brennan steadied the rifle across his arm and trained his eyes. Stretched across the field were the skeletal remains of a barn. But what happened to the light?

As if in answer, the ground became illuminated. Brennan turned as a towering figure swung forward.

Chapter Seventeen

Brennan blocked the blow of the circus-sized man with the stock of his gun then swung and clipped his chin. He tried to draw aim, but the undeterred opponent lunged for his gun before he could swing it into position. Brennan slipped from his huge grasp, but another assailant jumped him from behind, sending all three into the briars.

The barrel of his rifle clinked against metal as the fall thrust it from his hands. Brennan turned as thorns snared his shirt and grazed his neck and face. Hidden in the debris sat a steel strongbox, bearing the stamped names of Hobbs and Harts. One, two—three key holes graced the front in a horizontal line.

Entangled in the barbed underbrush, Brennan struggled to work free. He kicked his leg as one of the men grabbed hold and tried to yank him back. A weapon blasted from the clearing. Spurred by the heightened danger, Brennan tore through the briars and reached for his rifle. As his fingers made contact with the barrel it was ripped from his grasp.

A hand the size of his head clamped around the back of his neck and tossed him from the briars. Brennan stumbled forward and went for his sidearm.

"I wouldn't do that if I were you."

His frame tensed as he righted his gaze to a line of smoke trailing from the man's nostrils— Harris.

The fabricated deputy wagged a finger while one of his men aimed a rifle at Brennan's heart.

Brennan grimaced. "I should've known from the start. You're nothing but a gutless swine."

Harris's constant smile faded before he swung his fist into Brennan's face.

Brennan shook off the blow and smiled. "Such soft hands. Your mother must be proud."

Harris delivered another punch, this time barely rattling Brennan's teeth. Now he knew the strength of his adversary, or lack of. This one he could take lying down. It was the blonde gorilla that concerned him.

Harris turned toward the tall man. "Stretch, mount up and keep an eye out for the deputy. He can't be far behind."

Stretch. Familiarity coursed through Brennan. He hadn't recognized the man, but his name was well known. A villain almost as evil as Frank Ferris.

"He may not wake up 'til next week after the crack I gave him." The third man snickered, fitting Ruthie's description of a weasel.

Stretch swung a leg over his undersized horse. A buffalo would've been a better fit. "Have Dwayne take the other post." His voice rumbled like a roaring river.

"Don't forget who's in charge," snapped Harris. "Dwayne, bind the sheriff's hands. Then we'll talk about the key."

With his hands bound behind his back, Brennan followed Dwayne, the one he dubbed Weasel, while

Harris kept a gun to his back. As they entered the dilapidated barn, an owl hooted and soared from the rafters and out the door.

"Brennan?"

Angel's voice came with a wave of relief. Brennan struggled to keep from rushing to her side. The more concern he showed, the more Harris would use it against them both.

"Bring her out." Harris motioned to Dwayne.

As she stepped into the light, Harris shoved Brennan next to her. His shoulder bumped the wall of the stall behind her. Angel turned her face against his chest and whispered, "I knew you'd find me."

So much for not showing concern. With Angel close, Brennan couldn't control the urge to comfort her. With his hands tied behind his back, all he could do was place his chin on top her head then brush his cheek down the side of her face away from Harris. He whispered with the movement, "Are you hurt?" Trepidation toward her answer rippled through his veins as he strained against his rope bound hands.

"No."

"Enough with the sentiments." Harris pulled Angel back while the weasel snickered. "You might have fooled me with the puny amount of money in your bank. But that wasn't the only way I'd planned to make you pay."

His eyes narrowed. A vein throbbed in his temple as he spat, "Where's the key?"

Harris's sullied expression revealed his true nature. The man lived in constant fear. Fear of not getting what he wanted. Fear of those more powerful than him. Fear of failure. And before the night was over, he'd have a very real fear of Warsaw's sheriff.

Brennan's temper rose the longer Harris stood touching Angel. He needed a distraction. And thankfully, he was never at a loss for providing one. "What do you mean by a puny amount? Everything our town had was in that bank." A true statement. Harris and his men just failed to snoop in all the right places.

"I was there." Pride overrode Harris's controlled interrogation. His mouth pulled in a slow smile. "I was the one who detonated the dynamite."

"But not the one who collected, huh?" Brennan took satisfaction watching the smile fall from the villain's face. "Sounds to me your trained gorilla pulled the wool over your eyes."

Harris jerked his head toward Dwayne and pulled a gun from his holster. "You two robbed me?"

"Me?" Dwayne's eyes became huge as he jabbed a finger at his chest then toward the opening of the barn. "You had me starting the stampede even though you know horses make me nervous."

The man twitched his nose and stretched his neck toward Harris. "Maybe I was dealt the wrong hand. You and Stretch were the only ones at the bank."

The ease of the distraction gave Brennan little pleasure. Angel was still in the wrong hands. In a show of exasperation, he slid down the outside wall of the stall in a squatting position. If he kept them distracted, he'd have enough time to cut himself loose with his boot knife. "That's what's wrong with you criminal types. You're too quick to turn against each other."

"Enough! We all have a share to the *real* money." Harris whipped back toward Brennan, anger seething from his face. "Where's the key! And before you consider lying to me, know that the way she dies depends on your answer."

His eyes darkened with a sinister gloom. "Stretch and Dwayne spent a few seasons with my brother. I'm sure they'd be happy to share some clever ideas."

Brennan clenched his jaw. If only his hands were loose. He'd go for the man's throat.

"That's right. I figure a life for a life. My brother for the one who holds your heart." Harris fingered the gold locket around Angel's neck. "I assume he's the one you've been dreaming about, sweetheart?"

Angel swallowed and stared at her feet.

A deep rooted animosity heated Brennan's veins. He had to lead Harris away. He wouldn't let him hurt Angel. "The key's in my saddlebag."

"That easy, huh?" Harris cocked his head to the side. "And pray tell, where would that be?"

"I'll lead you to my horse."

Harris erupted in laughter then grew serious. "Dwayne will find him. Tell him where to look." He shoved Angel over to Brennan. Was this his trade for the information? Their last few moments together?

A damp wind whistled through the slatted walls as lightning lit the view outside the barn in a series of flashes. Angel slid to the ground beside him. Her body shivered then stilled. Brennan traced her gaze. Something moved outside, but the constant cloud-cover grazing across the moon obstructed his view.

Somewhere nearby, a horse snorted—Condor. It was the same sound the crazed animal made at soaring birds.

Brennan's first distraction, meant to give him more time, only succeeded in fueling distrust between the men. Now he was given a second chance.

"I reckon you'll get your answer soon enough. I heard him outside." With his knife now in his hands, Brennan leaned his head back against the stall as if bored with their indecision.

While Harris and Dwayne argued over who would scout for the horse, beads of perspiration formed along Brennan's hair line as he tried to keep a tight grip on the small knife and work the blade back and forth over the twine.

Within moments, an owl flew into the barn, followed by the drumming hooves of Condor.

The weasel man hollered and jumped to safety as the horse rushed past him. Harris shouted, "Stop him. He has the key!"

The mustang planted his feet and skidded to a halt halfway in the barn. He pawed the ground then turned a circle while gazing toward the rafters.

"Angel, slide back in the stall for safety." Brennan nudged her behind him and she inched her way into the dark corner.

Thunder rattled the sky and shook the atmosphere. A bolt of lightning struck a nearby tree shooting up a spray of sparks.

Dwayne's face contorted in fear as he fumbled for Condor's reins. The horse reared back and pawed the air. Dwayne made a garbled cry before a hoof raked across his head and knocked him to the ground. Condor snorted and shied away from the body then ran toward the entrance.

With the ropes nearly frayed into, Brennan snapped the remaining strings and freed his arms. As Condor rushed past, he flung himself toward Harris before he could fire. They toppled to the ground as the gun sailed out of reach.

Harris flailed and kicked beneath the sheriff's deadly hold. The thought of what he might have done to Angel fueled Brennan with barely controlled rage. He kneed Harris in the gut then drew him to his feet as if he were a rag doll. Harris sneered and whipped a hand from behind his back thrusting a blade toward Brennan's middle. Brennan shifted to the side and swung a hard knock to Harris's jaw. Stunned, Harris stumbled backward, his eyes blinking as if trying to focus. He sputtered and spit. Something fell to the ground. Harris's tongue ran across the front of his teeth, pausing at the gaping hole now left by Brennan.

"You're gonna pay for that." Harris wielded the knife and lunged again.

"Not likely." Brennan moved to the side while grabbing his wrist. He twisted it around Harris's back until the culprit's hand shook from pain and released the blade.

Brennan kicked the man at the side of his leg, instantly bringing him to his knees.

Harris breathed hard, air whistling through his new dental work. "You won't get away with this. Dwayne will ..." He squinted at his accomplice still motionless on the ground. "Stretch will get you. He'll make—"

"Dead men don't talk." Sheriff Douglas sauntered into the barn. The fire started from the lightening gave him a fierce silhouette.

Once again, Brennan was glad to be on the same side as the hardened lawman. He caught the cuffs tossed by his friend and restrained Harris's hands.

Flames licked at the side of the barn. Streams of smoke swirled between the boards robbing their oxygen. Brennan tossed Harris to Sheriff Douglas. "Take him. I'll get Angel then come back for the other one." He motioned behind him where Dwayne still lay unmoving.

Angel met him outside the stall, coughing from the fumes. Brennan swept her up in his arms and raced outside. The fire had greedily consumed the struck tree and the old privy leaning against its trunk. Flames lurched around the side of the barn making a path straight toward them.

"Brennan?" Angel's panicked voice rose above the roar of burning undergrowth.

Brennan whistled for Condor, not knowing if the horse was still close or if he'd ran for safety. Sheriff Douglas motioned from a safe stand of trees. Two other horses stood with his. Brennan hurried Angel to the other horseman. "Uncle Mike, take Angel and head to safety."

As he turned and ran back toward the barn, now engulfed with flames, Angel's protested cries were like a knife in his heart.

Brennan stopped long enough to tie his handkerchief around his nose and mouth then made his way toward the middle of the burning building. He gave a nervous glance overhead toward the creaking beams. If he didn't act quickly, both he and Dwayne would be caught in the inferno.

The smoke thickened, challenging each breath. Brennan hurried to where Dwayne had been knocked out. The floor was empty. He strained to see through the polluted air.

If the criminal had awakened, he undoubtedly found a way out. As the only plausible answer, Brennan accepted he couldn't do any more by staying inside. Crouched low, he began to retrace his steps.

The barn moaned and shifted its weight. Sparks flew as remnants of rafters burned free and fell to the ground. Brennan jumped back as one landed in his path. Flames shot to the side, igniting the interior wall beside him. More timbers splintered and cracked as the remaining roof gave a mournful cry before succumbing to its death.

Chapter Eighteen

Angel cried and wrenched against Mr. Hall's hold. "You can't leave him in there. He'll die!"

"Brennan knows what he's doing, Angel."

The man's words held little conviction as fire consumed the barn. "No," Angel whispered. *This wasn't part of my dream. God, don't let this happen.*

"It should've been you." Harris's words lisped through his toothless smile. "He should've had to live with the knowledge of how you were going to die."

"The fire's moving in." Sheriff Douglas turned his horse around, leading the other horse that held Harris tied to the saddle horn and the body of Stretch thrown across his back. "We have to move to higher ground."

"We can't leave him!" Angel jumped from Mr. Hall's horse. She dodged licking flames and made a wide berth toward the barn, running through a small stand of trees.

Thunder crashed overhead and a torrent of rain opened above. Her vision blurred by tears, Angel paid little mind to the needle-like pellets pounding her face. Bushes slowed her steps and caught her skirt, but none of that mattered. She couldn't lose him now. She loved him. Maybe she'd always loved Brennan, even when he was Juliann's. Though she'd kept her feelings secret then, Angel had envied her best friend.

At the edge of the forest, the rain suddenly stopped. Angel collided into something hard. She would've stumbled backward but a hand reached out and caught her.

"Brennan?" Hope lodged in her throat as she peered into the face of ... Dwayne. She screamed and twisted against his grasp.

"This ain't over 'til I get paid." He sneered and withdrew a shiny blade from a pouch at his side. "And if it ain't money, then I'll get it another way."

The sky continued to rumble as Angel eyed the knife reaching toward her throat. Her gaze flickered between the demonic eyes of her captor and his murderous weapon. Her heart thudded a rapid pulse as her throat tightened and threatened to cut off oxygen. She couldn't lose hope.

The blade caught the reflection of the burning building. Angel glanced from Dwayne and his snarl back to the knife. A sudden movement reflected in the steel. Like the Bible story of the men in the fiery furnace, a form emerged from the front of the barn.

Brennan!

A whistle sounded then he and Condor were racing toward them. A nervous rhythm trembled through Dwayne as hoof beats consumed the distance. His grip loosened and Angel wrung free. He blundered backward and tripped on a root, dropping the knife from his hand.

Condor came to a maddening halt. His nostrils flared, and he stomped the ground. Dwayne cried and covered his face with his arm. "Don't let him trample me!"

Brennan dismounted as steam rolled off his scorched shirt. He pulled Angel against him searing them together. She wrapped her arms around him and clung to his side. Brennan pointed the muzzle of his pistol at Dwayne.

"Get up."

Dwayne rose on unsteady feet, his nervous gaze dancing from the gun to Brennan's horse. With his hands on top his head, he led the way to the other men.

***

Brennan returned the next morning with Colton and Sheriff Douglas to the scene of the arrests. He scouted the forgotten property, trying to imagine what years of neglect now hid. The safe had probably been hidden inside the old house. But like the barn, age and weather had destroyed the structure leaving nothing but a patch of briars.

Sheriff Douglas cut a path toward the safe then glanced back. "Mind if I go first?"

Brennan motioned for him to go ahead. Each lawman held a key to the safe, taken from the three men they'd arrested. Gears clinked as Lincoln's sheriff took his turn.

Next, Colton stepped up to the safe and withdrew a key from his pocket. His serious expression couldn't hide the excitement simmering beneath the surface, just like in all of them. After he worked with his key, he stood back and stared at

Brennan. They both smiled. Today would put to rest several open cases. Justice would be satisfied and people could once again lay their heads on their pillows at night in peace.

Brennan inserted his key. Rust and debris fought against his hand as he tried to turn. Although he'd half expected this, his heart still pounded with frustration. "Come on ..." He wiggled it back and forth, hoping to dispel whatever hindered the gears. In slow motion, the key began to give, scraping against age and rust. Brennan tightened his grip and threw his weight behind his hand. The carrier turned and the final bolt slid back with a resounding clunk.

Brennan wiped his brow with his forearm, and drew a steady breath. The air grew heavy with anticipation.

He gripped the brass handle and pulled against corroded hinges. The steel door swung wide and every man gasped. Inside, a heap of gold bars gleamed beside the original paperwork, proving the rightful owners.

"If not for each man carrying a separate key, these would've been gone a long time ago." After an intensive night of questioning, Brennan had pieced together the story. Frank Ferris held up a train and found the safe secured on board. Trusting his men to shoot him in the back if caught holding all the keys, he quickly dispersed them, mailing his to an unnamed source—his brother, Henry—known to them as Harris.

"This is making me nervous just standing here." Colton took in the perimeter.

"I agree." Sheriff Douglas held out a burly hand. "Let's load the wagon."

"And quick," Colton positioned himself between the wagon and Sheriff Douglas, "or I'll be too late for my sister's wedding. And I don't want anyone else walking her down the aisle."

Brennan hefted one bar at a time and passed it behind him. After which, he and Sheriff Douglas moved the safe to the back of the wagon and reloaded the gold, locking it once again.

***

Outside the church, the day shone bright and clear with the sweet smell of hay ready to harvest. The wedding had been simple, but beautiful. Angel handed her bouquet of white blossoms to Clara before she smoothed the train of Emma's wedding gown across the short grass. Her kid-sister blushed beside her new husband, accepting the well-wishes of those in attendance.

Colton eased away from the crowd. Angel watched him make his way to their wagon. No doubt he was anxious to return to the solitude of home. He'd walked Emma down the aisle in place of their father, and though he wore a pleasant smile, Angel knew the celebration intensified the pain he'd battled since seeing Savannah off on the train.

Before the wedding though, a wire had come through. Angel couldn't wait for Brennan to tell Colton the news. Colton was needed in St. Genevieve, the very town Savannah lived, to transport a prisoner back to Warsaw's court.

Her brother's pain wouldn't last for long.

She stood back to assure Emma's train was straight as a hand brushed against her side. *Brennan*. She recognized his touch by her flush of emotions. She leaned into his embrace and gently skimmed his bandaged arm, knowing the worst burn lay across his shoulder.

For the first time, she understood Juliann's reluctance to give her heart to someone whose life was constantly in danger. Yet Brennan hadn't chosen his path out of selfish desires, but to help others. Angel couldn't hold his career against him any more than she could control the rapid beat of her heart whenever he was near.

She turned toward him. "Not all the gold in the world could replace you."

"Which makes you quite the catch, considering you're aware of the contents in the safe." He took her hand and led them to a private side of the church.

"Is your life often at serious risk?" Not that it would change anything, but the question had probed her mind for several days.

Brennan's eyes became a mask of trouble. His jaw clenched before swallowing. "Does your concern mean you can't marry a lawman?" he asked softly, sadness creeping into his voice.

"Marr—" Angel's heart thundered and stole her breath. Did he just propose? She blinked and realized with one simple word, everything she wanted would become hers. The man of her dreams, a beautiful home, the possibility of children.

Her answer trembled on the edge of her lips. She swallowed and ventured, "Do you think I'm what you need ... as a sheriff's wife?"

Brennan frowned. "If you can accept the risks." He stroked her face with the tips of his fingers, his features relaxing with the contact. "I love you ... more than I ever thought possible, but I am the sheriff—"

She leaned closer, tipping her chin. "You're my sheriff and I wouldn't want it any other way."

He dropped his head toward hers and everything else became a memory.
####

A Note from the Author

I hope you enjoyed reading Fourth Time's the Charm and the rest of the Warsaw series. Historicals are a great way to remind us of our great heritage and to be thankful for what we have.

Like many people from the Bible, Angel felt God had spoken to her through dreams, in fact, I believe He still does today. If my books do anything, I hope they ignite interest in the readers to delve deeper into Scripture and let God's Spirit reveal His majesty and wonder to their hearts.

I enjoy hearing from my readers and can be found at http://www.reginatittel.com, or you can leave me a message at reginatittel@gmail.com.

Also, if you enjoyed Fourth Time's the Charm, don't forget to read the rest of the Warsaw MO series and please consider leaving a review at amazon.com, or your favorite online store. Your encouraging words could be the catalyst someone else needs to purchase this book. Not only would you be sharing the Godly messages I shared with you, but you would also help promote me as an author.

Thanks again, and God bless!

Regina

Rivalry & Romance

In Mammoth Spring, MO, book one

by

Regina Tittel

"Uncle Frederick, we have to get that dog!"

Frederick winced as he took the stairs too quickly. He'd regret the action later. Ahead, he saw Miss Olivia Tolivar turn from the food stand.

"Boys," she called after them. Olivia knelt in front of Carl. In her hand was another sausage and bun. "What would you have done if you had caught that ole' mutt? Wrestle him for his treat?"

The boys giggled at her remark. Carl accepted the sausage while Curtis expressed their appreciation. "Thank you, Miss Tolivar. You're a lot nicer than Uncle Frederick says."

Frederick cleared his throat as his nephews ran down the street.

The gentleness Olivia had displayed toward the boys disappeared as she met Frederick's gaze.

"You acted too quickly, which doesn't surprise me." He reached into his pocket to retrieve another coin to replace what she had spent. "I was on my way over to answer the distress call— that was made for me."

Always the lady, Olivia kept from giving a heavenward glance. But he didn't miss her amber eyes narrowing as her mouth formed a taunt smile. "Aren't you tired, Mr. Sterling?"

"Tired, Miss Toliver?" He instantly straightened away from his cane.

"Yes, of holding your nose so high."

He stood speechless as she brushed past him and the offered coin. The fabric of her maroon-colored skirt swished with her movements.

***

Sparks fly between rivals Olivia Tolivar and Frederick Sterling.

As desk clerk of the Culp Hotel, Olivia longs to leave it all behind for the life of a wife and mother. The answer seems to present itself in the form of a visiting scholar. But can she accept their differences in belief?

When a shared passion to educate the less fortunate draws Frederick and Olivia together, Frederick's competitive nature vanishes as he begins to appreciate Olivia's strong mind and vulnerable heart. But will the results of his scheme to draw Olivia away from the hotel keep Frederick from winning her hand?

Now Available

In Warsaw, MO series

One Rusty Spur/Linda Cushman
http://www.amazon.com/dp/B00KQRUBII

Two Lonely Hearts/Mildred & Jonathan Colvin
http://www.amazon.com/dp/B00LU5AJUA

Three in a Quandary/Jamie Adams
(look for it soon!)

In Mammoth Spring, MO series

Rivalry & Romance/Regina Tittel
http://www.amazon.com/dp/B00DT4E4EW

Wishes & Whims/Jamie Adams
http://www.amazon.com/dp/B00DSD8WEW

Friends & Foes/Mildred Colvin
http://www.amazon.com/dp/B00EDVYO0Y

The Ozark Durham Series/Regina Tittel

Abandoned Hearts
http://www.amazon.com/dp/B004Z2KGEY

Unexpected Kiss
http://www.amazon.com/dp/B0063W0UIG

Coveted Bride
http://www.amazon.com/dp/B007ZHESP4

Cherished Stranger
http://www.amazon.com/dp/B00AOEVHQI

Devoted Mission
http://www.amazon.com/dp/B00HW2FYBE

Fourth Time's the Charm